Unlocked

(The Alpha Group Trilogy #3)

Maya Cross

This book is a work of fiction, the characters, incidents and dialogues are products of the author's imagination and are not to be construed as real.

Publisher: Maya Cross via Createspace
City: Sydney

ISBN-13: 978-1492809432

Dedicated to C.
For putting up with an awful lot.

A Note from the Author

I just wanted to give you all a little advanced warning that, while the first two books were purely from Sophia's perspective, Unlocked moves between both Sophia and Sebastian. It was something I wanted to do earlier, but I couldn't make it work without giving away too much. I hope you enjoy being in Sebastian's head as much as I did!

Chapter 1

Sophia

The first thing that I remembered was that I was cold. Everything was still black and my body wouldn't respond, but I shivered nonetheless. Then, gradually, things began to swim into focus, as though I were floating upwards from the darkest depths of the sea.

I coughed. Then again. And then sucked in several great breaths. One by one, I could feel muscles spark back to life. They were like dead weights, attached to my body, but at least I could move.

It took a few minutes for my mind to drag itself out of neutral. My first thought was that my lunch with Ruth must have turned into the bender to end all benders. It had happened before, and the cotton wool sensation in my head was at least a little reminiscent of my nastier hangovers. But then I remembered the following morning. My walk through Newtown. My newfound resolve to start getting things back on track.

The broken back door.

The stabbing pain in my neck.

The strong hands catching me as I fell towards the floor.

Oh Jesus. Oh fuck. What the fuck had happened? Where was I? And how long had I been out?

I flung myself into a sitting position, a move I instantly regretted as it sent a powerful coil of nausea twisting through my stomach. *Right, then. No fast movements.*

Drawing a few calming breaths, I steadied myself and surveyed my surroundings. At first glance, the room around me appeared fairly ordinary. Sparsely furnished, with just a bed, table, and bookshelf, the cream coloured walls and smooth wooden floor boards made it feel a lot like the guest bedroom in my parents' house. However it didn't take long for the differences to become apparent. Firstly, there were no windows, just a small space above the bed that looked to have been painted more recently than the rest. Similarly, the door looked somehow out of place; a giant slab of thick timber with a heavy iron lock.

Battling a bout of vertigo, I dragged myself to my feet and stumbled over to it. I knew what I'd find, but my chest still tightened when the handle refused to budge. The room may not have looked like a traditional prison cell, but it would hold me just as effectively.

This time, the nausea came on more strongly. It clawed at my insides like a wild animal. I tasted bile, sharp and hot, at the back of my throat. Somehow I managed to stagger to the corner of the room before my stomach emptied itself on the floor.

When it was over, I dragged myself back to the bed and curled into a ball. I knew I should try and approach the situation logically, but all I could focus on was the terror that was running like ice water through my veins. How could I possibly react rationally in the face of something like this? I'd been kidnapped from my house by unknown assailants, shot full of God knows what, and was now being held prisoner, for reasons I didn't understand. It was straight out of a horror movie.

Even through the haze in my mind, I knew that this had something to do with Sebastian. It was the only explanation that made sense. The fear I'd seen in that final letter told me all I needed to know. Whatever he was involved in was extremely dangerous, and now I was in the thick of it. And I had no idea why.

Take a deep breath, Sophia. Crying isn't going to do you any good.

I started with what I knew. They hadn't killed me outright. As horrifying as it was to consider, they could easily have done so. That meant they wanted something. Was someone trying to extort Sebastian? He certainly had the wealth for it. If that were the case, they'd probably already told him they had me. The ball was in his court. Would he do what they asked? It pained me to admit, but I didn't know. I had no doubt that he loved me, but the stakes were obviously much higher than I'd imagined. Perhaps they were too high.

Of course, extortion was probably the best case scenario. There were much darker possibilities. If Sebastian's secrets were as large as they seemed, it made sense that he'd have enemies, enemies who may be under the impression I knew something important. I suspected that if that were the case, they wouldn't be gentle about extracting the truth. My mind filled with terrifying visions; knives and saws and long iron pokers, heated to a glowing red.

Deep down I knew there was a third possibility too. Maybe my kidnappers weren't strangers at all. No matter how I approached it, I couldn't see Sebastian having anything to do with this, but I couldn't say the same for his colleagues. We hadn't exactly kept our discussion in his building private.

I knew Thomas had overheard and it certainly wasn't unreasonable to think that others might have as well. I had almost no idea what went on at Fraiser, a few scraps at best, but perhaps it was enough to make them feel threatened. And if that were the case, my gut told me that they wouldn't hesitate to do anything to rectify the problem.

I tried to convince myself that Sebastian was just moments away from tearing down the door and riding in on his white horse, but the truth was he had no way of knowing what had happened. He'd been very clear that all our ties were severed. Even if my captors had told him they had me, they wouldn't have been stupid enough to give away their location. For now, I was on my own.

Gradually, whatever they'd shot into me seemed to wear off and I began to feel more human. My mind ran in a constant circle, my body surging with some powerful combination of fear and anger. I paced the room, testing the lock over and over, searching for breaks in the plaster, anything that might hint at some chance of escape. I knew that it was all but impossible — this wasn't some hasty, spur of the moment snatch and grab — but I couldn't simply sit there and wait for what came next. It felt too much like admitting defeat.

I had no idea how much time passed. It's funny how quickly you lose sense of the hours in a room with no clocks or natural light. Eventually though, during one of my circuits of the far wall, there was a rattling at the door. Steeling myself, I took a few steps towards it and poised there. I wasn't sure what was coming, but I wanted to be ready, should an opportunity present itself.

The door flew open and a burly looking man in a suit walked through. He had dark olive skin, darker than Sebastian's, and heavy black curls that were cropped close to his head. He was carrying a tray with a sandwich and a glass of juice resting on it.

"Dinner," he said. He spoke with a sharp accent; Russian maybe, or Middle Eastern.

I had no doubt he wasn't the only one on guard duty, and judging by the easy confidence with which he moved, he wasn't particularly concerned about me escaping. But as he walked closer, I caught a glimpse of the open door behind him and all my survival instincts kicked in.

"Thank you," I replied, amazed by how little my voice was shaking. I reached calmly for the orange juice and began raising it to my lips, then with a flick of my wrist I tossed the liquid into his face and darted for the door.

In my head, it worked flawlessly. I saw him collapse to the floor as the citric acid set his eyes burning. I saw myself finding the guard outside sleeping on his chair and, after stealing his gun and handcuffing him in place, making a daring escape. Unfortunately we weren't in a movie. This was real life.

Instead of falling, my captor let out a short hiss, and one hand flew up to his eyes, but he was obviously well trained because despite his temporary blindness, he moved to block my path. In retrospect, it was a pretty stupid plan; there was only one place I could go and he knew it. But desperation is a powerful emotion and I only had two words running through my head at that moment. *Get away.*

I ploughed right into him. He must have weighed at least double what I did, but that didn't stop me from trying to fight. I let loose with everything I had, pounding his chest, his stomach, his neck. I landed a few good blows, but they barely seemed to register. It was like punching a mattress. The heavy muscle that coated his body absorbed everything. I shifted my focus, trying to strike him between the legs, but by that time his eyes were open once more and he blocked my attacks with ease, seizing my arms and pinning them together with one giant, meaty hand.

"Nice try," he said with a smirk. "Now, my turn." And then with almost derisive casualness, he flicked back his arm and struck my face with a colossal backhand. I spun through the air, my vision flaring white as I slammed into the floor. The impact knocked all the breath from my lungs.

"Eat," he said. "The boss wants to talk to you, but it may be a while." He glanced down at the now empty cup. "I guess you're going thirsty until then."

And with another smirk, he pulled the door closed behind him.

I crawled over to the wall and propped myself up against it. My whole head was ringing, and my cheek felt like it were on fire. It would be a lovely shade of purple in a few hours. *Great plan, Sophia. Just beat up Mr Universe over there and make a breezy escape. That'll work a treat.*

I knew I should probably eat, but just glancing at the sandwich made my stomach turn. How could I think about food at a time like this?

I desperately wanted to retain my composure, but that encounter had really driven home the hopelessness of the situation. I began to cry; fat, salty, desperate tears that flowed like a river down my face. I was utterly helpless. Escape was not an option. Whatever they wanted from me, they were going to take. The only question was how they would go about it.

* * * * *

Somehow, I managed to fall asleep. I don't know if it was the lingering effect of the drugs, or my body's way of trying to cope with the situation, but the next thing I remember is waking up to some sort of commotion in the hall outside.

I had no idea what it meant; the walls were thick and the sounds indistinct, but at this point, I assumed that any activity was probably bad. It signalled that we were progressing on to whatever happened next. I desperately wanted to hide, but there was nowhere to go. My chest felt impossibly heavy, and my heartbeat was like gunfire in my ears.

There was a brief lull, but after about thirty seconds of silence the lock jangled once more. I braced myself. The door flew open...

... and in stormed Sebastian, a sleek black pistol in his hand.

My stomach turned a cartwheel.

His face was a picture of desperation, fear etched into every line on his skin. Seeing him again made my whole body ache, the wound left by his letter tearing open inside me once more.

His eyes were wild, almost insane, but they lit up as they fell upon me. "Sophia," he cried, taking three quick strides and lifting me into the fiercest hug I'd ever experienced.

As he wrapped his body around mine, everything surged inside me. I finally let myself feel the full magnitude of the situation. I found that I was crying again. My chest shook with great heaving sobs, incoherent thanks spilling from my mouth. He was warm and strong and radiated control, and I buried myself deeper against him, as if his body could some-how shield me from everything I was feeling.

He took my reaction in his stride, holding me close and stroking my hair softly. "I know, I know. It's okay. I've got you."

His touch was soothing. His presence washed over me, filling me with that primal sense of security. I knew things were a long way from being okay, and I still had more questions than I knew what to do with, but at that moment, I'd never been more relieved to see another person in my life.

After some time, the flood finally began to ease and I found myself able to speak again. "Can we get out of here? I can't be here anymore."

"Of course."

As I pulled away, he caught sight of my face and his expression hardened. "Did they hurt you?"

"Well they did this," I said, gesturing to my cheek where I assumed a bruise was blossoming, "but that was mostly my own fault for trying to do a runner."

"None of this is your fault, Sophia," he said, sounding impossibly sad.

He led me out into the hallway. Somehow, I'd gotten into my head that Sebastian had done this alone, James Bond style; but, of course, that was ridiculous. Waiting for us outside were five hulking men, sporting earpieces and stubby black guns. Their crisp suits and grim expressions made them dead ringers for my visitor from before. If I hadn't known any better, I'd have guessed they were on the same side. *Maybe all the world's evil organisations shop at the same rental agency. Rent-A-Thug.*

But even my inner monologue's attempt at wit couldn't bring a smile to my face at that moment. Seeing them all standing there, alert and armed to the teeth, really drove home exactly what kind of shit I had embroiled myself in. They had guns, for Christ's sake. I'd never seen a drawn gun in real life before. Australian firearms laws are notoriously tough, so it's just not the kind of thing we are exposed to. But here were five men, carrying pistols as casually as if they were newspapers; and judging by the way they handled them, they were perfectly comfortable putting them to use. I couldn't see any sign of struggle in the hallway, but I doubted my captors had just invited Sebastian and company in for afternoon tea. Blood had been spilt here somewhere. Blood that, in a round-about way, was on my hands. I shook my head rapidly, trying to clear the image. That kind of thinking would do me no good.

Several men scouted ahead while the rest walked with Sebastian and I to the front door. It was dark outside, but judging by the suburban buzz in the air, it wasn't too late at night.

My prison turned out to be nothing more than a large, two-story house. Obviously some significant changes had been made, but to the casual observer, nothing would have stood out as strange.

There were several cars waiting for us. Sebastian guided me into one and followed me into the back seat, and in a matter of seconds we were turning the corner and pulling out into the night-time traffic.

Safety.

With every meter we put between us and the house, the tension in my muscles eased just a little more. I still felt like I might break down again at any moment, but at least the sense of sheer terror was subsiding. Now, I just felt exhausted, vulnerable, and utterly utterly confused.

Sebastian seemed to be almost ignoring me now. He was staring out the window, the initial relief on his face gone, replaced by a kind of heavy thoughtfulness. For my part, I didn't know what I was supposed to be doing. I was so ill-equipped to deal with the situation. Part of me just wanted to throw myself back into the comfort of his embrace, but now that we were making our escape, the questions began to come again, piling up in my head almost faster than I could process them.

"Where are we going?" I asked, figuring that was as good

a starting spot as any.

He looked over at me. "Somewhere safe."

"Safe from who?"

There was uncertainty in his eyes, that innate defensive-ness he'd spent a lifetime fostering. "Can we not do this now, Sophia? You've just been through one hell of an ordeal."

"Exactly, and now I want to understand what happened. So who the hell were those guys?"

His jaw worked wordlessly for a few seconds, but eventu-ally he let out a small sigh. "Honestly, I'm not sure."

"Seriously? No idea at all?"

He shook his head wearily. "We're working on it."

"Then how the hell did you find me?"

He hesitated. I could see what looked like guilt on his face. "After I sent you that letter... I know this looks bad, but I was worried about you. So," he drew a deep breath, "I left someone watching your place. It was just a precaution, but thank God I did. They saw the whole thing go down."

My eyes widened. "You mean you expected this?"

"No. No! Of course not." He ran a hand through his hair. He looked utterly distraught. "Like I said, it was a 'just in case' measure, that's all. Some of the people we deal with...well, there's not much they're not capable of, and things are a little unstable at the moment. I just wanted you to be safe."

"So why didn't your guy intervene?"

"There were three men that took you, and they were good - professional. He didn't think he could stop them by himself, so he called it in and followed, instead."

"I see." I couldn't say I wasn't thankful he'd had someone there, but it was a little like handing someone a fire extin-guisher after you'd set their place alight. Also, it drew my mind to the elephant in the room. Last time I'd gotten too curious, Sebastian had offered me nothing but heartbreak, but this was different. I was no longer merely a spectator. My life had been put in jeopardy. That entitled me to know a few things.

"How about we cut to the chase then. You may not know who they were, but you sure as hell know who you are. What kind of man are you, Sebastian? And what the hell is all this?"

He gave a desperate little shake of his head, his eyes darting towards the unnamed guard sitting in the driver's seat. "You know I can't answer that."

"So, what, I have to go along with all this without any idea what's happening to me?"

His brow furrowed. "I'm sorry."

I felt a surge of anger and I latched onto it. I may not have been able to take out my frustration on my captors, but I sure as hell could lash out at Sebastian. "Sorry? You're sorry? Are you for real? I just got kidnapped! Do you understand that? Sorry doesn't really cut it. Maybe in whatever secret, corporate world you guys play in that's normal, but in regular person land, that's kind of a big fucking deal."

He hung his head. "I know."

"At least give me something. What about a motive? I mean, what would anyone want with me? I have no idea about whatever it is you're into. As you just illustrated, that knowledge is clearly not for the likes of me."

His lips tightened. "I don't know exactly. We're trying to work that out."

I rolled my eyes. "Awesome. You don't know who they are, or what they want. Is there anything you do know?"

His expression hardened. "I know that I'm not going to let it happen again."

I gave a sour little laugh. "Forgive me if that doesn't fill me with confidence."

"What else do you want, Sophia? I'm sorry beyond words

that this happened, and I'm going to do everything I can to make it right."

Tears stung the back of my eyes but I forced them away. "How? How can you possibly make this right? There are people after me, Sebastian, and I'm guessing they're not going to stop just because you foiled them once. My life is officially in tatters and I don't even know why."

His mouth opened and closed but no words came out.

"You know, I lost my job," I said, after a few seconds of silence. My voice sounded strangely wooden, now.

For a moment, confusion flooded his face. "What? When?"

"A few days after I went to your office. Jennifer finally made her move." Surprisingly, I couldn't even muster much anger at her. My being fired already felt hazy, like a distant memory. "When it happened, it felt like the end of the world. All I could think about was the fact that I had to start from scratch. Now, I don't even know if I'm going to get that opportunity."

He looked like he'd been struck. "I promise that you will, Sophia. I'm going to get you through this. You'll get your life back."

"When? When will I be able to go back home and start rebuilding? When can I see my family? My friends?"

He glanced away and gave a little shake of his head. "I don't know, yet."

"That's what I thought. God, it seems like being in a relationship with you should come with an advance warning: may involve significant peril." Realisation slammed into me, and I rocked back in my seat. "Oh my God. Sebastian. The thing with Liv... was that like this?" I didn't know how it hadn't occurred to me earlier. The coincidence was impossible to ignore.

12

He closed his eyes and drew several long breaths, his fingers clenching into a fist by his face. There was something in that gesture that was stronger than mere anger, a kind of deep seated mental agony. "I don't know, exactly," he said, after a few moments. He spoke slowly, his tone soft and hollow. "We never arrested anyone. As far as we know, there was no kidnapping. It all happened in the house. Not a day goes by where I don't wonder about it, whether it was because of me." His face twisted in pain. I could hear him sucking back tears. "But this here, what happened to you, this is definitely my fault, and I know it's probably little comfort to you, but I'll never forgive myself for putting you in harm's way."

I stared at him, a torrent of conflicting emotions raging through me. Part of me was still furious. He had every right to feel ashamed. After all, if I'd never met him, none of this would have happened. He'd pursued me, despite knowing that there may be risks, and I'd paid the price for that.

But I couldn't ignore the anguish in his voice, the guilt that was etched on his face. He meant what he said about never forgiving himself. He would carry this forever. It was a strange role reversal, but suddenly I felt the urge to comfort *him*. Regardless of everything that had happened, I still hated seeing him hurt. The connection between us still blazed like an inferno inside me. It was like his pain flowed out through his pores and into mine, seeping into me.

I spent the rest of the trip gazing out the window, watching the houses roll by. My fear may have eased, but my confusion was at an all-time high. I still had no idea what I was involved in, but I knew it had to be big.

Whatever came over the next few days, I suspected that my life would never be the same again.

Chapter 2

Sophia

After driving for another half an hour we wound up at a giant old manor house, somewhere in the depths of eastern Sydney. It looked like the sort of place that belonged in a nineteenth century British period drama. A long driveway, manicured gardens, ivy snaking over the ageing brickwork like a network of veins. It was shielded from the outside world by a tall, concrete wall, with a Gothic looking wrought-iron gate providing the only access point.

"It's a secure location," Sebastian told me as we pulled in, although it was a somewhat redundant comment. One look at the expressionless men with automatic weapons, who were posted around the grounds, said that this wasn't somewhere you stumbled into uninvited.

A voice inside me wanted to know who the hell had multi-million dollar safe-houses just lying around for situations like this, but when stacked next to everything else that had happened, it somehow seemed to make sense. I felt a guilty little rush of excitement. Whatever world Sebastian had tried to keep from me, I was now being taken into the heart of it.

I'd decided to save the rest of my questions until we had a little more privacy. It seemed unlikely his friends would kidnap me, only to break down the door and rescue me a few hours later, but I was going to be cautious nonetheless. I was swimming in unfamiliar waters now. I couldn't afford any mistakes.

Sebastian and I hadn't said another word for the rest of the trip. There was something strangely distant about him now. It didn't make sense, but it almost felt as though he were angry at me.

Surprisingly, there were about ten people waiting for us inside, including several faces I recognised. Thomas and Trey both approached as I entered.

"What's with the welcoming party, guys?" I joked, bemused by their presence.

Thomas flashed a quick grin. "Someone called ahead. Said they'd got you. I'm glad you're okay."

"Yeah, you gave us one hell of a scare," said Trey.

"Well, thanks," I replied.

The two men shuffled awkwardly in place, their eyes darting to the floor. There was a strange tension in the air, and it didn't take a genius to figure out why. Whatever Sebastian's secret, the whole room was clearly in on it, and at that point it had to be obvious to everyone that I knew more than I was supposed to. I'd seen too much to still be in the dark.

Thomas and Trey appeared to be taking it in their strides, but not everyone looked so happy to see us. Several more of Sebastian's colleagues, including Ewan, were standing in a nearby doorway, assessing him with dark expressions.

"What's the deal with them?" I asked.

Thomas glanced over and grimaced. "Eh, just office politics. Don't worry about it."

Before I could delve any deeper, Sebastian appeared next to me. "There's a room made up for you upstairs. There's also food, if you're hungry."

I knew I should probably eat, but my stomach was still churning from the enormity of everything that had happened. What I really needed was a chance to process everything.

I shook my head. "I think I'll just hit the hay, if that's okay."

"Whatever you want," he replied.

I nodded farewells to the guys, who flashed tight little smiles before drifting back towards their colleagues. I wondered if they were going to get chewed out for talking to me. I got the sense that I wasn't exactly a guest of honour.

Sebastian led me upstairs and round the corner to a plainly made up bedroom. "There's a bathroom if you want a shower, and something to change into."

"Thanks," I said. That strange sense of hesitation was still there in his demeanour, like he was dealing with a distant cousin he only saw at family get-togethers. The desperation, the burning need I'd felt when he first burst into my prison, was nowhere in sight.

"Is there something else going on?" I asked.

"What do you mean?"

I nodded towards the foyer. "I'm not stupid enough to think they're all here for me."

He paused. "Things have been a bit crazy around here. Your disappearance... well, it wasn't an isolated event."

I wanted to ask more, but the way his brow furrowed and his voice shook when he spoke told me that perhaps the other situations hadn't turned out so well. There would be time to discuss it later.

He moved to leave, but paused in the doorway. "Like I said, this place is as secure as possible. You saw the guards as we came in, and nobody outside of us even knows it exists. You're safe here, Sophia."

I nodded, although it felt like a lie. In spite of the virtual fortress around me, I wasn't sure I'd ever really feel safe again.

* * * * *

In the past, I'd always considered sleep a sanctuary. A lot of people in high powered jobs struggle to get enough rest, but no matter how stressed or strung out I was, it had always come easily for me. I love that sense of complete escape, of just shutting down and blocking it all out for a few hours.

But tonight was different. Every time I closed my eyes, it was like being plunged into biting water. I kept remembering the way it had felt that morning, in my house, fading out as the drugs took hold. The brief explosion of dread like a hand closing around my heart as I realised, too late, what was coming. Suddenly the darkness of sleep wasn't soothing, it was terrifying.

And every time I did manage to drift a little, I always woke in a cold sweat, just minutes later, a montage of terrifying images playing through my head. I hated that sense of powerlessness. I was the one in charge of my mind, dammit. The experience had been horrifying, but now it was over. There was no reason to let it affect me anymore. But logic didn't seem to be relevant. This was beyond rationality. Something had broken inside me.

The third or fourth time I woke, it was with a sob. Moonlight cast the room as a series of jagged silhouettes, and despite knowing I was somewhere safe, the unfamiliarity of my surroundings sent something sharp skittering through my chest.

Suddenly, it felt like everything was closing in around me. I let out another cry and burrowed deeper under the covers, feeling fresh tears welling in my eyes. I didn't want to be this person, this person who cried at shadows, but I didn't know how to deal with the emotions that were roaring up inside me.

I felt another bolt of fear as I heard the door open, but in a moment there was a familiar weight on the bed, and then Sebastian's arms were circling my body from behind.

"It's okay," he said, his voice soft. "Let it out."

I have no idea how he knew I was in distress, but in spite of everything that was still unresolved between us, I loved that he'd come. The sheer strength of his presence dwarfed everything else, dulling the fear. He was my rock and I clung on for dear life, lest I slip back below the surface again.

He didn't say anything else and so neither did I, but just the act of being together was enough. I lay there, listening to the sound of his breathing, enjoying the sensation of that solid chest rising and falling against my back. Gradually, my turmoil began to dissipate. I had no idea how he had such a calming effect on me. When we were together, nothing else seemed to matter.

He felt like home, and for just that night, I pretended like he still was.

Chapter 3

Sebastian

I hadn't expected Sophia to sleep at all, not after what she'd been through. Trauma like that can break a person. But somehow she'd drifted off. I had no idea where she found the strength to be that tough. She never ceased to amaze me.

For a while I lay there, trying to get some rest myself, but the events of the last two days had thrown my whole world into chaos. It was all happening again. The fact that I'd averted the worst didn't make the situation any better. I was an asshole. I should never have let it get to this point, but I was weak, and it had nearly cost the woman I love her life. How the hell could I sleep, knowing that?

To make matters worse, even now I couldn't stay away. She was as secure here as anywhere, but the moment she'd left my sight I began to feel agitated. I still hadn't managed to shed the mindless terror that had seized me when I first heard she'd been taken. The urge to go to her, to simply hold her and never let go, had been almost overpowering.

I'd tried to distract myself. There was certainly no shortage of work to be done — most of my colleagues were holed up together in the board room, planning well into the night — but I was useless there. My mind only wanted to focus on one thing, and soon I found myself sitting, propped up against the wall outside her room, nursing several fingers of scotch in a heavy crystal tumbler. I didn't know why, but just being close to her helped. I made myself vow not to enter. It had taken an immense level of control to cut her off the first time, and every moment in her presence stretched my willpower just a little more. I would keep her safe and solve all this, and then when it was all over, I'd let her go again. It was the only way.

But the moment I heard her sobbing through the door, all sense of self-control fled. Before I knew it, I was on my feet and in her bed. I expected her to fight, after all, I had to be the last person she wanted to see, but she didn't. Instead she just burrowed into me without a word. I hated how perfect that felt, the way her body fit like a missing puzzle piece against mine. I still didn't understand how such simple contact could make me so content, but it did.

And now she slept. I couldn't help but run my eyes over her again. Truth be told, I'd barely been able to stop staring since the moment I entered the room. She looked so fucking beautiful lying there, her face utterly peaceful, her curves perfectly accentuated by the thin cotton sheet. She'd taken the T-shirt I left her, but not the pants, and now in the throes of sleep she'd managed to knock part of the cover free, exposing one delicate hip. It was a tiny thing, the barest hint of pale skin and black cloth, but the sight took my breath away nonetheless. I felt impossibly low, ogling her after everything I'd put her through, but I was powerless to do anything else. Her body was like a drug, a burning rush through my system that was impossible to ignore. I knew how that hip would feel, if only I'd reach out and touch it. I had every inch of her body charted in my head; so perfectly soft, so perfectly feminine.

Fuck. I had to pull myself together.

Ripping my gaze free, I eased my arm out from under her. I'd done what I came to do. She was resting. There was no reason for me to stay.

She stirred briefly, and I came within a hair's breadth of pulling her back against me once more, but after a few moments she settled. Taking one last look, I moved quietly out into the corridor and resumed my watch. I'd be there if she needed me, but anything beyond that was too hard. There was no happy ending here, and letting myself think otherwise would only destroy me more.

* * * * *

I spent the entire night in that hallway. After a few hours my back was killing me, but I refused to move until the sun rose. It was stupid — there were many men much more dangerous than I, stationed around the complex — but I felt compelled to guard her personally, just that once, like that could somehow make up for my earlier failure.

At around seven, I heard her stirring. Not wanting her to know about my vigil, I slipped downstairs and headed for the kitchen. I'd sent enough mixed messages for one night.

I had no idea what the day would bring. Ever since I'd heard about her kidnapping, I'd been operating purely on instinct. A kind of base fury that blotted out everything else. But now that I had her, I had to face the reality of the situation. Now the fallout would begin.

She came downstairs while I was eating breakfast. She looked impossibly angelic; eyes bright, hair tussled. God, no wonder I was in trouble where she was concerned. Even first thing in the morning, frightened and bruised, she was utterly gorgeous, and every time I saw her, it was like seeing her again for the first time.

She shot me a small smile, but it was cautious, deflated. I didn't blame her. "Hey," she said.

"Hey," I replied. "Sleep okay?"

She nodded, apparently unsure if she should say anything about my visit. "Eventually, yeah. I'm starving now though."

"I expected you might be. There's toast or cereal. I'm sorry it's not scrambled eggs, but we're a little unprepared here."

She blinked a few times, her expression unreadable. I don't know why I made reference to that morning. It felt like a lifetime ago.

"That'll be fine," she said, and set about making herself something. A minute later, she joined me at the table.

We ate in silence for a while, but I knew that was temporary. She had that glint in her eye again, and the curious little curve of her mouth that I'd seen so many times before. It was the first thing I'd noticed, months ago, when she snuck into our party. I'd known that curiosity was dangerous, but somehow when I opened my mouth to send security after her, I found myself dismissing them instead. The worst part was that, even now, I couldn't make myself regret it.

"So," she said, after a few minutes. "What happens now?"

I grimaced. I didn't know what to tell her. All of this was unprecedented. Her very presence here went against every rule in the book. "Now, we try to find who did this."

She nodded slowly. "And what about me?"

"You'll stay here until it's safe for you to go home."

She stared for several seconds. "And that's it?"

I shrugged and nodded.

"You're still not going to give me any kind of explanation?"

I knew it was pointless, but I tried to fend her off nonetheless. "Like I told you before, Sophia, these secrets, this life, it isn't mine to share. Nothing about that has changed since I wrote that letter."

Her jaw tightened. "Nothing has changed? Are you kidding me? I just got kidnapped, Sebastian. Kidnapped! If that doesn't change things, I don't know what does."

I didn't know how to reply. She was right. Of course she was right. But that didn't give me license to break two millennia of tradition. "I'm sorry," I said, but even I knew it sounded weak.

"That's not good enough. It was one thing to keep me in the dark when it was just our relationship on the line, but it's more than that now. This is my life, for Christ's sake. I didn't ask for this, but like it or not, I'm here now. I deserve to know what the hell I'm involved in."

I stared into my coffee. There were no right choices. If I told her, I'd be betraying my brothers. But if I didn't, I'd be betraying her. She wasn't going to take that lying down either. If I didn't give her answers, she'd try to find them on her own. And who could blame her? If I were in her position, I'd want to know. But if she started digging, it would only make things worse.

"This isn't a secret like other secrets, Sophia," I said, feeling impossibly heavy in the chest. My heart and my brain continued to wage war inside me, but I think the battle was already decided. I wanted her to understand why I'd made the decisions I'd made, why I'd caused her such pain. "This isn't the kind of thing you promise to keep to yourself, then get drunk and spill to your friends."

She rolled her eyes. "I kind of figured that when it caused

a couple of men to break into my house and drug me. I get it, this is serious business."

I exhaled slowly and glanced towards the door, realising exactly how dangerous this was. Most people were still asleep, but all it would take would be one early riser to overhear, and both of Sophia and I would wind up in the firing line. The severity of everything else that was going on here had allowed me a little leniency with the rules, but that would only extend so far. Sharing our secrets was one of the most serious breaches possible.

I got up and checked the corridor, then shut the door. "You can't let the others know I told you. I mean that. They're not stupid. They must already realise you know more than you should, but there's a difference between suspicion and confirmation. If they even catch a hint of this discussion, they'll have grounds to take the matter further, and at that point I doubt I'll be able to protect us."

Her breathing quickened a little, and for a few seconds I could see her wrestling with herself, but eventually she gave a quick nod. "I understand." I couldn't help but smile. Told that this information could get her killed, she barely blinked.

I closed my eyes. I felt a little like I was about to jump out of a plane. "I'm... part of something," I said. "Something very old and very big. We're called the Alpha Group."

"That's what the 'A' stands for?"

"Yes."

She nodded to herself. "Okay. So what is it?"

"It's tough to describe. The best phrase would probably be a secret society, but thanks to Dan Brown, that now conjures up images of religious cults and portals to other worlds. The truth of it is a little subtler than that."

"A secret society?" she said, enunciating each word carefully. She didn't look surprised, in fact she seemed incredibly calm. "Like the Freemasons?"

"Kind of, but not really. These days, they're more of a social club than anything else. It's difficult to be a secret when everyone knows you exist."

Her eyes were focused intently on me, quietly processing every word I said. "So, what do you do that's so different?"

I gave a wry smile. "That's not easy to summarise. We have our fingers in a lot of pies. In a nutshell, we try to steer things in specific directions."

"What sort of things?"

"Whatever we think is important," I replied. "You have to understand, this isn't some two-bit little operation, Sophia. What you've seen here is the tiniest fraction of the group as a whole. We have people all over the world. Government, finance, entertainment, you name it. Each member is carefully selected for the influence they bring to the table and, through that network, we can pull whatever strings we want."

She closed her eyes briefly, pinching the bridge of her nose between two fingers. "I'm not sure I understand. I mean, I knew you had to be involved in something big, but this is some conspiracy theory stuff you're claiming." She shook her head slowly. "So, what, are we talking like rigging elections and starting wars?"

I licked my lips. "Those are pretty extreme examples. We tend to be a little more low key than that. I'd rather not go into the specifics — I'm breaking enough rules as it is — but everything we do has a larger purpose."

"And who decides on the larger purpose?" she asked, a hint of disapproval in her voice. "If what you're saying is true, aren't you basically just a group of people who conspire to use your connections to do whatever the hell you want?"

"It's a little more complicated than that. You're judging us without knowing anything about us."

"So explain it, because it seems to me that a group like this is basically corrupt by definition. No wonder you and your friends are richer than sin."

I sighed. It was almost impossible to make her understand in the space of a single conversation. People were normally brought in slowly, over a matter of months. It had taken me nearly a quarter of a year to fully wrap my head around it all. "It's not like that. Most people in the group are recruited *because* of their wealth and power, not the other way around. The group is fundamentally about doing good."

"In what way?"

Apparently I was going to have to give more details. I wracked my brains for an example that would get through to her. "Remember the town I told you I grew up in?"

She nodded.

"Well I made that my first project when I joined, before I came to Australia. The group worked wonders over there. We got the government to pave actual roads, had them install better water filtration, even got the town on the electricity grid. It's still dirt poor, but the people there actually have a chance now. Our work isn't all that overtly philanthropic of course, don't think I'm sugar coating it, but our overall goal is to fix glaring inequalities, to protect people who can't protect themselves."

"But those sorts of responsibilities belong to the government. You know, the people we actually *choose* to run things."

"Come on, Sophia. Someone as smart as you can't really believe in the effectiveness of the government when it comes to protecting the individual. There's as much corruption there as anywhere in the world. Look at the GFC. Millions of people were financially ruined, and yet nothing came of it. Nobody has really been punished, no changes have been put in place. And that's just the tiniest tip of the iceberg."

She pondered this. "Okay, that might be true, but if you're so concerned with the lives of the everyday worker, why didn't *you* do something about that?"

I grimaced. "That's a sore spot for us, actually. The truth is we just didn't see it early enough. We're powerful, but we're not omniscient, and the big banks are particularly hard for us to break into at a high level. The kinds of guys who are happy to swindle people for billions aren't generally the sort of members we want to recruit."

For a few seconds she sat in silence, her face impassive.

"You know me," I continued. "You know the sort of person I am. Is it so hard to believe we might actually have good intentions?"

Her expression softened, although she still seemed somewhat unsure. "Let's say I believe you," she said. "There's still a lot of questions unanswered. Like how are you not discovered?"

I shrugged. "We're very good at staying under the radar. We've had a lot of practice. The group is over two thousand years old."

Her eyes widened. "Two thousand?"

I nodded. "This sort of thing doesn't just spring up overnight. We started in ancient Greece — hence the name — as a way to keep the government in check, and it kind of grew from there. Democracy was new then, and there were... teething problems. When those problems didn't go away with time, we hung around. Anyway, with the amount of influence we've now got, keeping our activities out of the limelight is actually fairly easy, as long as we don't do anything too bold."

"So what about Fraiser Capital then?"

"It's a real company," I replied, "but it's also our main front, here in Australia. Venture capital firms throw money at all kinds of strange projects. Having it as a legitimate entity makes financing and directing our operations much easier."

"So that party I snuck into...?"

"A meeting for potential new recruits."

She nodded to herself. "Right." She was much calmer now that the initial disbelief had worn off, calmer than I'd expected.

Her eyes flicked to mine, and she hesitated. "So I'm guessing that a group like this probably has its share of enemies," she said slowly.

I could see where she was going with this, connecting the dots. "We do."

"Enemies that might do things like kidnap your members' girlfriends?"

My shoulders slumped. "It's possible." Instinctively I reached out to clasp her hand, but managed to stop myself. *No more mixed messages.* "Believe me, I've been wracking my brains trying to work out why this happened. I have no idea what anyone would hope to gain from taking you."

"Is there anyone out there that might want to hurt you personally?" she asked.

It wasn't like I hadn't been through that a thousand times too, both now and when Liv was killed, but I always came up empty. "Not that I can think of."

She pondered for a few more seconds. "What about whatever's going on here then? The other disappearances. Is there a connection there?"

I closed my eyes briefly, feeling a fresh surge of anger. With everything that had happened to Sophia, it was easy to forget that there was more at stake than that.

"Maybe. Those situations were a little different," I replied, struggling to keep my voice level. "They weren't disappearances. They were murders."

Her hand flew to her mouth. "Oh God," she said, and

this time she was the one that reached for me. That simple contact felt wonderful and, although I knew I should, I didn't pull away.

"The first one happened a few days ago. Charlie didn't show up for an appointment. We didn't think too much of it, until the next day, when someone went to his house and discovered his body."

"Jesus," Sophia replied.

"We were still trying to figure it out, but then yesterday, the same thing happened with Simon. At that point we knew we were under attack, so we followed protocol and gathered our senior members here." It felt strange to be saying this stuff out loud. It made it seem more real. I'd known Charlie and Simon for the better part of ten years. They were my friends, and although saving Sophia had briefly blotted out everything else, I felt their loss as keenly as anyone.

"I'm sorry," she said.

I nodded in thanks. "Perhaps there's a connection there," I said. "Perhaps it was the same people and we just got to you before..." I couldn't finish the sentence. "Anyway, we're using every available resource to work out who is responsible. And I swear to you, I won't stop until you're safe and you can leave all of this behind."

She stared at me for what felt like an eternity, her jaw set tightly, her eyes flickering with some emotion I couldn't identify.

Eventually, I heard the sound of a door closing upstairs. People were starting to wake up. Realising she still held my hand in hers, I reluctantly pulled away and got to my feet. "I have to go. There will be a meeting soon and I have to prepare. Just try to lie low, okay? I'll check in with you later."

She gave the barest hint of a nod.

I felt better, having told her the truth. Now she understood. It didn't make up for the pain I'd caused, but it was something.

On my way back to my room, I ran into Trey, who was just coming in through the front door.

"Just the man I wanted to see," he said. He wasn't part of our senior council, so he wasn't staying in the house. He was out on the street, working leads and keeping the rest of Alpha's ventures running smoothly.

"Oh yeah? What's up?" I asked.

He handed me a file he was carrying. "Just got these back from our team. None of those guys that took Sophia came back with any kind of match. Whoever they were, the computers of the world do not know them."

I let out a long sigh. Everything we'd run so far on Sophia's kidnappers had come back negative. Nobody should have been that hard to track. We had access to every database that mattered.

"Thanks," I said to him. "Keep at it. Something has to give eventually."

"Will do." He hesitated, like he was afraid to ask what came next. "How's Sophia doing?"

I gave a weary shrug. "I don't know. It's hard to tell. I think she might still be in shock, to be honest."

"Yeah, I can imagine all of this is pretty difficult for a civilian to process."

"That's one way to put it," I said heavily. I had no idea how she was going to react to everything I'd just told her once she had some time to digest it. It could go a thousand different ways. "Anyway, I should go. Meeting in a few minutes."

"No worries."

I turned to go, but then a thought occurred to me.

"How do you do it, Trey?"

He cocked his head to one side. "Do what?"

"Keep your private life and your professional life separate?" A few years ago, Trey had been just like me. One empty fling after another. But then he'd had his own Sophia moment. He'd met a girl who made him give all that up, but unlike me, he managed to keep her in the dark. I didn't think I'd even met her. He kept her totally separate from anything group related. I always wondered how he pulled that off.

He flashed me a half smile. "I just have a girl who understands me, I guess."

He made it sound so damn easy.

Chapter 4

Sebastian

I'd always known there were protocols in place for if a situation ever got really bad, but I'd never experienced them first hand until now. All of our key personnel were currently gathered here in lock down. It was part strategy meeting, part protection detail. We couldn't afford to leave ourselves exposed, not when we were completely on the back foot. Whoever was behind the attacks was clearly well connected. So far, they'd been like ghosts.

After a quick shower, I headed to the back of the house. We'd set up a makeshift board room in the study, and the bulk of the inner council was already there when I arrived. Thomas, and one or two others, nodded greetings, but the rest either ignored me or scowled pointedly before turning away. I hadn't done myself any favours rescuing Sophia the way I had. It went against several key group rules, and a good chunk of the room wasn't in a hurry to let me forget it. If the situation had been any less dire, I'd probably have faced disciplinary action; but, for now, they had to settle for dirty looks and snide comments. We had bigger things on our plate.

"How you holding up?" asked Thomas, coming over to join me.

I shrugged. "How do you think?" I tried to keep the frustration from my voice, but I didn't do a very good job.

He studied me for several seconds. "You got her out, man. That's what matters."

"Is it? Then why do I still feel like shit?"

"Hey, I don't blame you. I'd be angry too. But try to go a little easier on yourself. You couldn't have known."

I felt my hands contract into fists. "Of course I could have. You know, I really thought I was smart enough not to put anyone else in this position again, but apparently I'm a slower learner than I thought."

He flinched a little at my tone, but his voice remained calm. "I thought we were past this. You know as well as I do that the situations are completely different. What happened to Liv was a tragedy, but there's nothing tying it to any of this. It was a freak accident, that's all. You have to let it go. Stop blaming yourself."

I gave a bitter little laugh. It wasn't like I hadn't tried. Objectively, I knew he was right. Our investigation had never found anything to indicate that Liv's death was more than a standard break and enter gone wrong. But no matter how much evidence there was to the contrary, the heavy sensation I'd carried in my stomach since that day refused to dissipate.

From the moment Liv and I became something more than a casual fling, part of me had felt uneasy about it. There's no hard and fast rules about relationships within the group. As long as our secrets remain hidden, you're allowed to do whatever you want. Most Alpha members simply choose to forgo that kind of companionship to make their lives easier, and I'd been firmly in that camp. Then I met her.

Liv had a vibrancy to her that was completely infectious. I'd never known anyone like her. She was passionate and energetic, and she seemed to genuinely care about me for more than just my money. In retrospect, I could recognise more than a little youthful infatuation in our relationship, but at the time it felt like something deeper. A little voice in the back of my head constantly told me that I was leading her down a dangerous road, but I was too selfish to stop. I don't know why I was surprised when it blew up in my face. Even if her death *was* an accident, I still broke her heart, and I hated myself for that. I swore I'd never be responsible for that sort of pain again.

But now there was Sophia. If my attraction to Liv was the firm pull of a magnet, my attraction to Sophia was like gravity; unyielding and inescapable. Something about her just rendered me utterly powerless. From the moment I met her, I felt like I was trapped in a whirlpool, swimming in vain against the current as it gradually sucked me down. It scared me. It felt like only a matter of time before it drowned us both.

"Either way," I said, "I still put Sophia in danger. You're not going to try and absolve me of that one too are you?"

He sighed. "Just because you're involved doesn't make it your fault."

I wished I could believe that. He was just being a good friend, but no amount of support could fix this.

I gazed around at the roomful of men I'd given my life to. From the moment I joined the group, they'd been the world to me. Even when I was with Liv, I'd never considered a different path. "Do you ever regret all this?" I asked, my tone softening. "Because I have to say, right now, for the first time, I'm actually starting to doubt my choice."

He flashed a sympathetic smile. "I think we've all felt like that, at one time or another. This isn't an easy road, by any means. But you know how important it is."

I nodded, though it was more for him than me. Truth be told, I wasn't sure I knew what was important anymore. Nothing made sense now.

A few minutes later, everyone had arrived. We took our seats.

"So," said Ewan, "give me some good news." Although he wasn't in charge in any real sense, as the longest serving member, he ran the meetings. He was also the most visibly upset person in the room. Sunken eyes spoke of sleepless nights, and his hands roved restlessly across the table, as if just staying in motion might somehow speed things up. The two men we'd lost, Simon and Charlie, had been close friends of his.

Marcus, the youngest member of the group, grimaced. He was our point of contact for the investigation. "We don't know much more than yesterday, unfortunately. Our guys went over every inch of Simon's house, but it was the same as Charlie's. No signs of forced entry, security footage wiped. Whoever it was did one hell of a job."

"What about the autopsy?" asked Thomas.

"Still coming," replied Marcus. He glanced at Ewan. "He didn't go gently, though, I can tell you that much."

Ewan slammed his fist down on the table. "I'll make sure *you* don't go gently, you little shit."

"I don't mean to be disrespectful," replied Marcus, looking a little pale. "But it's important. This wasn't just about taking them out. Someone went to a lot of effort working them over, which means that, chances are, they wanted to know something."

"Were the two of them working on any projects together?" I asked. "Anything tying them together?"

But before Marcus could reply, Ewan cut in. "Well, look

who has decided to rejoin us," he said, making a big show of looking surprised to see me. "Does that mean you're ready to focus on what's important again?"

"I'm sorry about my absence last night," I replied, trying to remain calm. "I had other things on my mind." He was right to be angry, and if I'd been in his position, I'd have reacted the same way. I had an obligation to these men, an obligation that couldn't just be cast aside on a whim. But the suggestion that anything was more important than finding Sophia made everything inside me tense.

"That's exactly my fucking point," the older man replied. "We've got a major crisis going on, and your head isn't in the game. It's busy burying itself between a pretty pair of thighs."

Thomas' hand flew out, firmly holding me in my chair. He knew me well. Rage poured through me. "If you keep talking like that," I said, my voice sharp enough to cut glass, "the group will be down another member before too long."

"Is that right?" Ewan asked. He didn't look even slightly perturbed. "You'd put her before one of your own? You're even further gone than I thought."

Guilt and anger seethed in my stomach. Ewan and I had never gotten along, and I knew most of his aggression was just frustration at the loss of his friends, but there was a tiny part of me that thought he might be right. Perhaps my priorities really had changed. "Why do you care so much what I do?"

He laughed. "You flatter yourself. Honestly, Sebastian, I don't give two shits what you do. But what I do care about is you using Alpha resources to rescue your girlfriend when they could be out there finding the bastards that did Simon and Charlie in."

I opened my mouth, unsure exactly what I was going to say, but Thomas jumped in ahead of me. "You still don't think there's a connection there, Ewan? The people that took

Sophia were organised, efficient, and clearly backed by some serious money. Exactly the sort of operation that might have been able to take out our guys."

Ewan shifted uncomfortably in his chair. "That doesn't prove anything."

"That's true," Thomas said, "but it is a pretty big coincidence, and I, personally, don't care much for coincidences. In any case, we have very little idea what's going on here yet. Let's not lose our heads until we know more."

Ewan seethed in his chair for a few moments. "Maybe you're right. Maybe. But you want to hear what I know already? I know that the group is under attack, and yet there's a civilian girl walking around in our headquarters, seeing everything, overhearing God knows what." He turned his gaze to me and raised his eyebrows ever so slightly, as if to say, 'Or being *told* God knows what.'

"Where do you want her to go?" I asked, desperation creeping into my voice. "You know the kinds of people we deal with. Sending her back out there may well be a death sentence."

For a moment, I thought I'd gotten through, but then Ewan's expression hardened further. "I don't know, but she doesn't belong here."

"For now, I say she does," Thomas said. "At least until we know what we're up against. Someone wants her, and if it *is* the same people who did that to Simon and Charlie, then it's in our best interests to deny them what they want, wouldn't you say?"

Ewan glared around the table. Several others seemed to share his disapproval, but nobody could come up with a counter. It was hard to argue in the face of sound logic.

I shot Thomas an appreciative smile. "I'll make sure she stays out of everyone's hair," I said to Ewan.

He nodded curtly, and the meeting turned to other matters. Despite my best intentions, however, I couldn't focus. All I could think about were Ewan's words. In truth, he was right. Bringing her here had been a mistake. Even if I'd told her nothing, her curiosity would eventually have gotten the best of her. The moment she'd walked through those doors, everything had changed. But all other paths led to the unthinkable. I didn't know what other option I'd had. It was a no win scenario.

* * * * *

I spent the rest of the day alone in my room, trying a few more abstract methods to identify Sophia's kidnappers, but the truth was, it was mostly a waiting game at this point. All the information we had was already out there. We were just waiting for someone to get back to us with something positive. It was incredibly frustrating. We had all the power in the world at our fingertips, and we were still coming up empty.

At about five in the evening, there was a knock at my door.

"You got a minute?" asked Marcus, poking his head inside. It had ruffled a few feathers that we had promoted him to the council so quickly, but despite being relatively young, he was a really promising member; the perfect combination of smart and level-headed.

"Sure, what's up?" I said.

He stepped inside and closed the door behind him. "Well, I just got something back from the lab, and I thought you should be the first to know."

I felt a tingle of excitement. Maybe we'd finally caught our break. "Tell me you've got a name for me," I said.

He licked his lips nervously. "Not exactly. Our guys are

still trying to run down who exactly owns that house you raided. Whoever it is laid one hell of a paper trail. What we did get was a match on some blood we found in one of the rooms there." He hesitated ever so slightly. "It belonged to Simon."

I sank back slowly into my chair. Thomas had been right, the two situations *were* linked. I wasn't surprised — the coincidence was difficult to ignore — but knowing for sure only made our predicament more confusing. Why would anyone go to pains to kill two of my brothers, but then take Sophia instead of me? All I could think of was that they wanted leverage over me somehow, but I couldn't imagine what for. It was baffling.

"I appreciate you telling me first," I said.

"No problem. The others called a pre-dinner meeting, but I kind of figured you might not show."

I nodded. "Yeah, I might sit this one out. You've given me a lot to think about." As much as I wanted to be there to see Ewan's face when the connection was confirmed, I didn't particularly feel like wading back into that minefield just yet.

"No worries. I'll keep you posted."

"Thanks."

I sat for a while after he left, pondering the new discovery. As frightening as the situation was, in some ways that connection was a good thing. Whatever our enemies were planning, Sophia was obviously a part of it, and so rescuing her had likely thrown a spanner in the works. And since we now had just a single target, I could feel comfortable directing the full brunt of Alpha's resources at the problem.

It was little progress, but I knew Sophia would want to hear about it anyway. I found her in her room, curled up on the bed, nursing a cup of tea and staring at the wall.

"Hey," she said, as I entered.

"Hi." Our conversations were uncomfortable now, like the lies and secrets had piled up to form an invisible barrier in the air between us. It was what I wanted, it was what *we* needed, but it still hurt like hell.

"How are you holding up?"

She shrugged. "As well as can be expected, I guess. There's not much to do around here." She held up her mug and gave it a little shake. "Although this tea addiction I'm developing looks promising. This is my fifth cup today."

"That stuff will kill you," I said, managing a small smile.

She returned it, and something loosened in my chest. "So they tell me. Anyway, how's the big investigation? Assassinate any presidents today?"

"Not that I know of, although that's not my department," I replied. I was glad she was still able to find humour in the situation. Maybe she wasn't quite as damaged by it all as I'd feared. "I did get one small piece of info, though."

She gazed at me expectantly. "Yeah?"

"They found a few bloodstains in that house you were being held in. Our lab just matched it with Simon, one of my brothers who was killed."

Her expression grew tense once more. "I see. I guess the connection makes sense. Does that help you find out who's behind it?"

I shook my head. "We're still coming up empty on that, so far. But now that we know the investigations are linked, we'll be throwing everything we have at it."

She nodded, although she didn't look particularly comforted. "Okay."

"There's something else I wanted to talk to you about," I said, moving over to sit next to her on the bed. "I know this situation is awful for you, and God knows that being in this place isn't making it any easier."

"You mean the friendly Scotsman and his band of merry men?" she said.

"Yeah. I know they're not the most welcoming lot, so I was thinking, what if you went away for a while? We have the resources to get you a new passport, a new identity, and obviously money isn't a problem. You could go wherever you wanted, and nobody would be able to track you down. It would be kind of like a holiday."

Part of me hated the idea of sending her anywhere I couldn't watch over her, but my argument with Ewan had got me thinking about alternatives. Her presence here was certainly problematic, and it wasn't going to get any easier. In fact with everyone on such short fuses, it felt almost inevitable that something would explode eventually. This wasn't a world she belonged in, and taking a trip was the only way I could think of to extricate her while still keeping her safe.

"And how long would I be gone, exactly?" she asked, her expression unreadable.

"You know I can't give you an exact time frame, Sophia."

I thought she was going to blow up at me, but when she spoke, her tone was calm. "I appreciate the offer, but I have a life here, Sebastian. The idea of dropping everything and disappearing with no return date in mind doesn't sit well with me."

I closed my eyes, feeling a huge stab of guilt. Whether or not she went, her life was on hold. She could hardly wander back home in a few weeks if our enemies were still out there.

"Just think about it, okay?" I said.

"Okay."

She continued to stare at me. There was a sadness to her expression, but also a glimmer of something else, something questioning. I realised then how closely we were sitting. There was barely a foot separating us. Her smell — orange blossom

41

and vanilla — suddenly seemed to be everywhere. All I had to do was lean in and my mouth would be on hers. I could already visualise how she'd taste, how she'd tremble, how her tongue would feel curled around my own.

I knew I should leave, but my muscles refused to obey. All I could do was sit there and drink her in. Fuck, I wanted to kiss her. I wanted to grab hold of her and push her down and show her that she was still mine. But, of course, that wasn't true.

I didn't understand why she hadn't sent me away yet. Instead she just sat with her eyes locked to mine, her lips hanging ever so slightly open, like an illicit invitation. There was something smoky lurking in her gaze now, something that shouldn't have been there.

It was almost enough.

Closing my eyes, I sucked in a shuddering breath and got to my feet. "I have to go."

She was still for a few seconds, then nodded slowly. For a brief moment, I almost thought she looked disappointed. It didn't make any sense.

I fled.

I needed to be alone with my thoughts, but as I headed for my room, I ran into the last person I wanted to see.

"Sneaking in a quickie while the rest of us are slaving away, hey?" said Ewan, who was waiting for me around the corner.

"I'm not in the mood, Ewan," I said, trying to swerve around him, but he stepped sideways, blocking my path.

"Maybe I am," he said.

I found myself fuming at his school boy antics. "Have you got something you want to say?"

He chewed thoughtfully for several seconds, as if working an invisible piece of tobacco around his mouth. "Marcus filled us in on what he'd found. Looks like your girl *is* involved in all this, somehow."

"Does that mean you're going to get off my back about it?"

He laughed. "Hardly. Just because you went and created a weak spot for yourself doesn't mean the group should have to clean up after you. Having her here is a liability. We don't know her and we don't trust her."

"I trust her."

"Do you?" he asked, bitter amusement evident in his voice. "Perhaps that's the problem."

I took a step closer, feeling something animal flare in my chest. "What's that supposed to mean?"

But Ewan was not easily intimidated. "It means that something here doesn't add up," he said, staring me right in the eyes. "Nobody outside of Alpha should even know the council exists. Yet a month or two after you start swapping promise rings with Ally McBeal in there, suddenly our guys start dying."

"You're joking, right? Did you forget that they took her too?"

He gave a little shrug. "Maybe they were just finishing the job. Cleaning up loose ends."

It took every fibre of my being not to knock him to the floor. My hands twitched at my sides, both balled tightly into fists. But I was already walking on thin ice as it was. Hitting him would only make things worse.

"This is ridiculous," I said.

"Maybe. Maybe I'm way off. But either way, there's no excuse for breaking the rules."

I stared at him with gritted teeth. There was nothing I could say. He was right and we both knew it.

Not knowing what else to do, I moved to leave again.

This time he didn't try to stop me. He'd gotten his message across. Sophia's presence here was more than an inconvenience, and it was only a matter of time before she was out on her own.

Chapter 5

Sophia

The second night was a little better than the first, but not much. More than once I woke flushed and sweating, the sharp tang of my latest nightmare still fresh on the back of my tongue. I wondered if this was post-traumatic stress. Based on what little I knew, it certainly seemed possible. I'd never understood how you couldn't just block that stuff out, but now I did.

Part of me expected Sebastian to magically appear once more and slip into my bed like a comforting ghost, but the door remained closed. I found myself disappointed about that. It seemed crazy to think about the prospect of 'us', in the context of everything that was happening, but no matter how terrified and out of my depth I felt, there was no denying the strength of my feelings for him. Not to mention my attraction. The energy that had sprung up between us when he'd visited earlier had nearly overwhelmed me. He had this way of looking at my body, like he was preparing to devour me, that ignited something deep in my stomach. I wanted to be angry — hell I *was* angry — but if, at that moment, he'd kissed me, I wasn't sure I'd have put up a fight.

I didn't know whether to be touched or offended at the 'holiday' he'd offered. It did feel a little like he was just taking the easy route and trying to sweep me under the rug, but at the same time, everything he said was valid. Things were uncomfortable here, and I knew it must be just as bad for him. I appreciated the predicament he was in, even if it was somewhat his fault. I just wished I wasn't in it as well.

More than once I considered agreeing to go. An all-expenses paid trip overseas was hardly the worst proposition in the world; but, truth be told, the idea of being out there all alone scared me. My life was here and it was under siege. I couldn't just run away while somebody else dealt with that.

After several hours of restless turning, I gave up trying to sleep and reached for my phone. Sebastian hadn't mentioned it, but when I woke up that morning, I found a few of my possessions waiting for me in the hallway outside. Apparently he'd sent someone to my house.

It was a good thing too, because there were already several texts from the girls waiting for me. Another day or two and they'd have started to worry.

Ruth: Hey Hon'. Hope the wallowing is going well. If you need another pick-me-up, I'm willing to take one for the team and suffer through a few more midday mojitos. Let me know.

I'd read them over and over today, relishing that tiny connection to my old life. It had been less than two days, but somehow that's what it felt like now: my old life. At a time where everything else was in ruins, it was nice to be reminded I still had someone waiting for me when this was all over. If it ever would be.

I'd already reassured them both I was fine, conjuring up some story about visiting my sister down in Melbourne for a little mental recharge, but as I stared at the screen now, I was nearly overcome with the desire to call them and tell them everything. It was a terrible idea, but curled up there, in the unfamiliar dark, surrounded by people I barely knew with agendas I couldn't even fathom, I felt so incredibly alone.

After staring for a few precarious seconds, my thumb poised over Ruth's number, I shoved the phone back into my bedside drawer and headed out in search of tea. What I really wanted was something a little more numbing — I figured a house like this had to have a wine cellar — but drinking away my problems probably wasn't the best option right now. I needed to stay alert. The world seemed to have turned into a much more dangerous place, virtually overnight, and in this dimension of secret societies and covert kidnappings, waking up with a killer hangover might have a different meaning entirely.

I had no idea how to process everything Sebastian had told me. Part of me wanted to laugh it off as an absurd joke, something dug out of a bad eighties espionage film, but taking into account everything that I'd seen, I believed it. I didn't know what it all meant yet, but I planned on remedying that situation. As unbelievable as it was, I was a part of this, now. I could either sit, awestruck on the sidelines, or I could try and work out exactly what the hell I'd gotten myself into.

The house was silent as I made my way to the kitchen. It wasn't until I put the kettle on and began hunting for a cup that I realised I wasn't the only person awake.

"Can't sleep?" said a voice behind me.

I nearly jumped out of my skin. Turning, I saw a familiar figure, cast in shadow, nursing a mug of his own at the breakfast table.

"Jesus, Joe. You scared the hell out of me."

He chuckled. "My apologies," he said, although he didn't sound particularly sorry. "Feel like some company?"

It seemed harmless enough. I wasn't exactly going to drift off anytime soon. I filled my cup and moved over to join him. "I take it you know what happened?" I asked.

He nodded. "I was there when Sebastian got the news."

"Then you know why I can't sleep."

He nodded again. "I don't blame you. I don't think anyone would rest easy after a thing like that."

I appreciated that he didn't offer any advice. Just understanding.

We sat in silence for a few minutes. Despite the lack of conversation, I was enjoying the company. He might not have been Sebastian, but his presence seemed to hold back the darkness a little nonetheless.

Eventually though, he spoke. "He told you." It wasn't a question.

Fear seized my belly. I turned my gaze to him slowly. He didn't look angry, in fact a ghost of a smile touched his lips, but I knew what he meant nonetheless. It hadn't occurred to me that Joe might be an Alpha member. He just seemed like hired help. But clearly there was more to him than that.

I debated denying it, but the certainty in his eyes said there was no point. He knew. The question was, what would he do with that knowledge?

I let out a long sigh. "He did."

Joe chewed his lip thoughtfully. "Well then."

"You don't sound surprised."

He shrugged. "Everyone likes to think they can keep their mouth shut when necessary, but the truth is, every man has his breaking point. The way he talks about you, the only thing that surprises me is that it took this long."

The way he talks about you. My mind instantly went back to Sebastian's letter, to all those heartbreakingly sweet things he'd said. And then to that look he'd worn when he first pushed his way inside my prison, the rapture that had lit his face when his eyes found mine. I wasn't the only one struggling to switch off my feelings.

You always hear stories about the purity of love, about the way it swells inside you until nothing else even matters. I never cared much for that perspective before — that kind of love typically isn't compatible with the sort of future I saw for myself — but now I found myself longing for it to be that simple. Every decision had turned into a conflict, a titanic battle between heart and brain, between logic and emotion. I couldn't deny my feelings for him, but whenever they rose inside me, they brought with them anger and betrayal. I knew it wasn't intentional, but he'd exposed me to this world, a world that was currently trying to chew me up and spit me out again. It was hard to forgive that, with the terror of my kidnapping still blanketing everything like a thick fog.

And even if I could get past it, there were other elements to the equation. Was he still the same man I'd fallen for? In light of everything he'd told me this morning, I didn't know. It was almost easier to just write him and his friends off as corrupt, power hungry monsters; but, try as I might, I couldn't see him being a part of something like that. Not to mention guys like Thomas, or apparently Joe. If Sebastian said their intentions were noble, then I believed him.

"This is a mess," I said, after a pause, not sure if I was referring to my relationship with Sebastian or the forbidden knowledge he'd shared.

Joe let out a laugh. "That it is, girl. That it is."

"So you're a member too then?" I asked, stalling for time. I wasn't sure where the conversation was going exactly, but he'd obviously brought it up for a reason. Something in my gut told me I could trust him, but Sebastian's warning loomed large in my mind nonetheless.

"Indeed."

"Well, I don't mean any disrespect, but isn't it a little demeaning having you drive another member around?"

He shrugged. "It's not so bad. I give him hell, but Sebastian's a better sort than most. Besides, it's not like I always did this."

"Oh?"

He grinned. "Alpha's not exactly in the business of recruiting chauffeurs. Not much to be gained by that. No, before this I served thirty years in the British Army."

I nodded. That explained the war wound he'd mentioned the first day we met. "In what capacity?"

"Infantry first, but they quickly shuffled me to the officers' path instead." He leaned in conspiratorially. "Didn't seem to care for all the questions I asked." He let out a short laugh. "Nope, there's not a lot of space for curiosity on the battlefield. I think they figured that if I was going to be doing all that thinking, I might as well be the one answering the questions instead of asking."

"I think that's fair enough," I replied.

"That's actually where I met Sebastian."

"Sebastian was in the army?" That revelation reminded me exactly how little I knew about the man who had stolen my heart.

"Briefly." He gave a rueful shake of his head. "He was a terrible soldier, just like me. Too headstrong, too stubborn. I was his commanding officer, and it got to the point where I was forced to discharge him, but it seemed like such a waste. There was something special about him. I knew he was capable of doing great things, and the characteristics that made

50

him unfit for duty made him perfect for Alpha. So I released him from service and nominated him for consideration to join the group. He was accepted, and now here we are."

"I see," I replied, trying to picture Sebastian in mud spattered combat fatigues. It was difficult. The suit and tie seemed almost like his second skin.

"What about you? Why'd you quit?" I continued.

"Well, obviously I had more important things to do here," he deadpanned, nodding in the direction of the bedrooms.

I laughed. "Obviously."

"Honestly though, I just kind of got tired. You'd think gaining rank would be a good thing, but by the last decade of my career, I dreaded it. Every promotion meant a little more time spent behind a desk, a little more paperwork. There was nothing to look forward to, anymore."

"And so your solution was to drive your protégée around, day in and day out?" I asked.

He shrugged. "It may not seem particularly exciting, but the truth is, there's rarely a dull moment around here."

Thinking back on everything that had happened in the last few days, I could see his point. If this sort of stuff was a regular occurrence, I wasn't sure my heart could keep up. Another point against Sebastian and I ever having a real relationship. Thinking about it gave me a newfound respect for military wives. The prospect of my partner constantly venturing into indescribable danger was daunting, to say the least. I didn't know how they coped.

"Is it always like this?" I asked. "Kidnappings and secret lairs?"

He smiled. "Sometimes, but not as often as you'd think. These are pretty dire circumstances. Most of the time it's more like being a politician; lots of paperwork and meetings."

51

"So Sebastian just has impeccable timing then."

Joe stared at me for several seconds. "Don't be too hard on him, Sophia. He didn't mean for any of this to happen."

I let out a long breath and shook my head slightly. "I know, but it doesn't change the fact that it did."

"Not to downplay what you've been through at all, but to be honest, I think he's dealing with it as badly as you are. Like I said, I was there when he got the news. I've never seen anything like it before. He could barely speak. Everyone seemed to take it as anger, but I know him better than most. I knew it for what it really was. Fear.

"He wanted to throw everything we had at that house the moment they took you there, but that's not how the group works. You can't just use Alpha resources for personal situations, no matter how serious they may be." His lips compressed. "They argued for hours. Virtually the whole room was against him. Eventually, he realised they weren't going to budge, but rather than back down, he just stormed out and came for you anyway. Took an entire squad of our troops. To be honest, I'm kind of glad nobody physically stepped in to stop him. I have little doubt he'd have gone by himself, if he had to.

"For now, nobody is doing anything about it. We've got too much else to worry about. But if I know that group, he hasn't heard the last of it. Not by a long shot." His gaze bored into me. "I understand that this was hell for you, I really do, but Sebastian did everything in his power to make up for what happened. He put himself at risk to save you, so maybe cut him a little slack, hey?"

My mouth felt impossibly dry. I knew Sebastian had been distraught at my kidnapping, but this cast it in an entirely new light. He hadn't simply been cleaning up an Alpha group mess. If anything, he'd been doing the opposite. He'd actively put my safety above the interests of his brothers. He'd broken the rules for me. I didn't know what it meant — was it a temporary lapse or a permanent statement? — but it made me warm all over. My mind was suddenly racing with possibilities.

"I didn't know," I said eventually.

"Well, now you do," he said with a nod.

"Will he be in serious trouble?"

"I don't know. Time will tell. But, in the past, such actions have been... frowned upon, let's just say."

Something about the way he said gave me the impression it was more serious than he was letting on.

I weighed his words. Were Sebastian's actions enough to overcome all of the lies and the secrets? I didn't know. I still had so many questions.

"Liv's death," I said carefully.

His expression turned grim. "Now that was a hell of a thing."

"Sebastian said nobody really knows what happened. Is that true?"

Despite his age, he was still sharp. He saw my implication instantly. "You're wondering if he should have expected this?" He shook his head. "No, nobody could have seen this coming. He blames himself for Liv, but the reality is it was just a case of wrong place, wrong time."

"But if there was nothing to worry about, why did he leave someone outside my place?"

"Paranoia I suspect. You have to understand, Sebastian took that hard, harder than anything I've seen, until you disappeared. He feels like if he hadn't ended things with her, if he'd found some way to make the relationship work, perhaps things would have been different."

I blinked in surprise. "Ended things? He told me they

were engaged."

"Ah," he said with a wince. "I'm sorry. I assumed he'd told you the whole story. Technically he didn't lie; they were engaged. Several of us tried to warn him of the dangers of such big secrets in a marriage, but it's hard to argue with love. Of course, it became progressively easier as she began to get suspicious. She was a bit of a computer guru, you see. Was being headhunted by all kinds of A-list companies, but they wanted her to move overseas and Sebastian couldn't, so she turned them down. Anyway, one day, Sebastian left his laptop open at an Alpha login portal. To most people that wouldn't mean much, but to a girl like her, it was a beacon. Soon, she was digging up all manner of strange info. It wasn't enough to tell her anything concrete, but it told her he was hiding something."

He took a long sip from his mug. "So, she confronted him. They argued and she gave him an ultimatum."

"And he chose the group," I finished.

He nodded slowly. "Although 'chose' might be a little generous. This isn't the sort of thing you can just walk away from. A few people have managed over the years, but it requires an immense amount of planning and a willingness to drop totally off the grid. Not exactly an appealing prospect for an up and coming IT whiz."

"I guess not." It was a lot to take in. I couldn't help but notice all the parallels. As well as the one big difference. Sebastian had initially chosen the group this time too but, when push came to shove, he'd picked me.

"Anyway," Joe said, dragging himself to his feet, "it's time to take these old bones to bed. It's been lovely chatting with you, Sophia."

"Goodnight."

He moved to leave, but paused in the doorway. "I hope

that whatever comes of all this, you find some peace."

"Me too," I replied.

Chapter 6

Sophia

I intended to head back to my room but, instead, I found myself walking right past the door and continuing up the hallway. Something told me that Sebastian would still be awake. I didn't know exactly why I wanted to see him, only that I did.

My instincts proved accurate. I found him sitting at a desk in his room, hunched over a laptop screen. The door was open, but he didn't appear to notice me, so for a while I simply stood and watched. He looked tired. No, that wasn't the right word. Haggard was more appropriate. A man with the weight of the world on his shoulders.

Even now, just the sight of him sent a tingle curling through me. A surge of lust, but there was something deeper too, something comforting and strong that blossomed in my stomach like a sunrise. It made the prospect of seeing him again exciting, no matter how often it happened. I was beginning to think that feeling would never go away.

I tried to put myself in his shoes; impossible obligations

pulling at me from all sides. Would I have reacted differently? Would I have continued our relationship, knowing the world I was exposing him to? I didn't know. It felt like a position where there were no right moves.

"I know what you did for me," I said eventually.

He flinched at the sound of my voice, his hand darting towards the desk drawer, although he stopped when he recognised me. "Christ, Sophia. Sneaking up on people at four o'clock in the morning in this particular house is a really, really bad idea."

"Sorry."

He studied me. I could tell that part of him simply wanted to send me away. Every conversation between us now was difficult, strangled by guilt and uncertainty. But eventually he spoke. "What do you mean, what I did for you?"

"The way you stood up to your brothers when no one else wanted to help rescue me."

He waved dismissively. "Ah, that. It's not a big deal."

"That's not what Joe said. He said it was quite the argument."

I walked inside and sat on the surface of the desk. Sebastian was close enough to reach out and touch now, and I had to resist the urge to do just that. I was doing a good job of keeping my fear at bay, but that didn't mean it had fled. It still simmered inside me, waiting for another opportunity to boil over, and the prospect of facing that alone was almost too daunting to consider. Just being near him soothed my shredded nerves.

"You broke the rules for me," I continued. "In a pretty big way, from what I understand."

His gaze was hard, radiating intensity. I could almost feel the conflict playing out inside him. "What else could I have done, Sophia? I couldn't let them take you."

"I thought the group came first."

He hesitated, then shook his head slowly. "So did I."

We sat in silence for a few moments. I think we both knew what was coming. We couldn't avoid discussing our relationship forever. I was still afraid to do so, lest that wound tear open inside me again, but knowing what he'd done gave me a glimmer of hope. Maybe, somehow, there was a way through this.

"Sebastian, I—"

"Don't," he said, rising to his feet and putting some distance between us. "We can't do this, Sophia." His voice was sharp, almost pained.

"I have to know," I replied. "What does all of this mean for us?"

He stormed towards me and I jolted backwards. "There *is* no us. There can't be. You've seen the sort of life I lead. How can you even ask that?"

"I don't know," I said softly. "But I'm asking all the same."

He closed his eyes and swept a hand through his hair. "I nearly got you killed. I don't understand how you're even still talking to me."

A few days ago, I might have agreed with him. Logically I knew I still should. But logic had always taken a back seat where he was concerned. Yes he'd kept things from me, but I now appreciated the full weight of those secrets. Everything he'd done spoke of how much he cared for me, and I couldn't deny that my emotions burned just as strongly. I could hold the situation against him, or I could move on and try to build something to go back to, after it was over.

"I don't blame you, Sebastian. I did in the beginning, but I don't now. You couldn't have known. Yeah, if I hadn't met you, none of this would have happened, but then I'd never have met you and, the truth is, that thought terrifies me far more than any of this."

He stared at me with wide eyes, his expression hovering somewhere between anguish and awe. "How do you do that?" he asked. It was barely more than a whisper. "No matter what I do, no matter how sure I am, you say just the right thing to make me question myself."

A smile crept onto my face. "I'm just that talented, I guess."

His expression softened a fraction, but it didn't last long. "I can't keep making these mistakes, Sophia. It's too dangerous. Sure, I saved you this time, but what about next time? Or the time after? This life offers no guarantees. I won't give it another opportunity to claim you."

"So that's it, then? I don't even get a say?" Moisture rushed to my eyes. "Don't my feelings count for anything?"

"Of course they count," he lamented, although he didn't seem to know how to finish the sentence.

"So if we never had a chance, why tell me all those things then?" I asked. "Why bring me into your world? Why slip into my room at night and comfort me like nothing has changed?"

He shook his head desperately. "I don't know. I don't know."

For a few moments there was silence.

"Do you remember what you said to me over dinner, the first time we went out?" I asked eventually. "'Nothing worth having comes risk free.' Well, that's how I feel now." I got to my feet and moved over to him, taking his hands in mine. "I'm a big girl. I can make my own decisions. I understand the risks, and I'm telling you I'm okay with them. I love you, Sebastian, and if that's the price for being with you, then it's one I'm willing to pay. The question is, are you?"

The surge of emotion on his face mirrored my own. That

was the first time I'd said the L word out loud to him. It hadn't been intentional, but the moment it left my lips I knew it was true. It was so perfectly right. I could feel it down to my bones.

He closed his eyes momentarily. "You have no idea how long I've wanted to hear you say that. But not now. Not now!" Pulling his hands free, he turned away. "I don't know if I can keep fighting this, Sophia. It hurts too much. Seeing you every day, not being able to hold you or kiss you or love you. It's ruining me."

"So stop fighting."

For a few seconds, I thought I'd lost him again, but then he was spinning and his lips were crashing into mine.

I'd never been kissed like that, not even by him. In that gesture, I could feel every ounce of his guilt, his pain, his love, and I found myself kissing back just as ferociously, my own torrent of emotions thundering through my chest. The joy I felt was almost enough to make me weep.

In a few seconds, he'd worked my track pants free and lifted me back onto the desk. No words were necessary. Desperation and longing burned brighter than the sun in both of us. I needed that connection, that perfect affirmation that said more than words ever could.

I was dimly aware that the door was still open, but nothing in the world could have stopped us at that moment. We were utterly lost in one another. With raw hunger, he yanked his fly down, freeing his shaft, and then buried himself inside me. My skin burned with the suddenness of it, but I didn't care at all. I savoured the pain because it came from him, a stinging symbol of the bond between us.

He moved slowly, coaxing my body to life around him with gentle thrusts. I mewed softly against his mouth, feeling myself grow slick, but he didn't break the kiss. He devoured me, drawing my lips tenderly between his teeth and stroking them with his tongue. His hands found my legs, looping under my knees to lift them higher, allowing him to sheathe himself in me all the way to the root.

Finally he pulled away, only to bury his head against my neck. "Say it again," he whispered, teasing me with a slow rocking motion.

"I love you," I breathed.

"And I love you," he replied.

And then he was moving in me again, his mouth tracing fire across my collarbone, sending my capacity for speech spiralling away. His thrusts strengthened as the animal in him gradually broke free of its cage. He snarled against my chin, one hand slipping between my legs to find my clit, sending a new chord of ecstasy thrumming through me.

His lovemaking was different now. Every time before, I'd seen a new side of him; sometimes dominant, sometimes soft, sometimes hungry, but this was all of those things together; fierce strength combined with loving tenderness. I felt like I was finally getting all of him, no more shields, no more secrets, he was finally letting it all go, and it was the most beautiful thing I'd ever experienced. In that moment I knew that I was his and he was mine.

As his rhythm reached its crescendo, the pressure building in my core began to swell. I wrapped my hands around his neck, fingers digging into his flesh, his body tightening in time with mine as we came together.

"God, I've missed you," he said, laying his forehead against mine as we caught our breath. Standing there above me, dishevelled and bathed in sweat, he looked absolutely radiant.

I nuzzled my nose against his. "Me too."

We moved over to the bed and lay, for a while, in each

other's arms. The bliss I felt in that moment almost made it possible to forget everything that had happened; we were just an ordinary couple, snuggling together, after making love.

"I love you," I said again, turning to stare him in the eyes.

He smiled. "I'll never get sick of hearing that." His expression slipped a little, and I knew we were about to come hurtling back to reality. "I hate to break the moment, but we aren't done talking. If we're really going to do this, there's some things we need to think about."

"Okay," I replied cautiously, half afraid he was going to go off the deep end again.

He took his time choosing his words. "Even when we get through whatever is going on right now, I don't know exactly how we make this work." He raised his hand to cut off my objections. "I'm not saying we don't try. I can't deny this anymore, Sophia. I love you, and for some stupid reason you appear to return the feeling."

"I'm a slow learner, I guess," I replied.

He shot me a half smile. "The fact is, you're here and you're involved and you know things you shouldn't know. And my brothers... some of them are already worried about you. They're distracted now, but when things settle down, and we're still together, they're going to start asking questions of their own, and I don't think they're going to like the answers."

I'd been wondering about that. I may have been saved from immediate danger, but the longer I spent in the Alpha house, the more I realised that I wasn't as safe as I'd thought. I couldn't just forget everything I'd seen, and these people knew it. "So what do we do?"

He shook his head. "I don't know."

"You kind of make it sound like we're doomed, no matter what."

"No, no, that's not what I meant." He exhaled sharply. "I'll figure something out. For now, we just need to tread carefully. We both know a lot of people don't approve of your presence here, so let's not give them any reason to take it further."

Once again I felt an uneasy feeling settle in my stomach. "Are you sure about the people who kidnapped me?" I asked carefully. "Because if there's any chance it was someone here, we might wind up playing right into their hands."

"I'm sure," he said firmly. "These men are my brothers. Besides, whoever took you also killed Charlie and Simon. Nobody here would do that."

His certainty put my mind at ease; well, as at ease as was possible with some kind of rogue terror group trying to kidnap me. "You've used the word 'council' a few times," I said, spotting another chance to sate my curiosity, "is that like the Alpha board or something? I've been trying to work out how you make your decisions."

His jaw tightened a fraction. "I'm not sure I should talk about that."

"Oh come on. They're already going to be super angry if they find out what you've told me so far, right? So how much worse can it get?"

He hesitated, but eventually gave a resigned smile. "I guess you have a point. Yeah, in a nutshell, the council runs things in this area; it's in control of the Asia Pacific region. Other regions are run by different groups."

"And you're on it?"

He nodded. "Almost everyone here is, except the muscle, drivers, and house staff."

"So that makes you kind of a big deal, then?" I asked with a grin.

He laughed. "Kind of."

It made sense. I struggled to picture Sebastian anywhere but the top of the ladder, regardless of what he was doing.

"So it's like a democracy? You all just vote on everything?"

"Yes and no. For most decisions, the whole council has a say, but ultimately there still needs to be a figurehead, to settle disputes and keep the group operating smoothly. The official title is Archon."

"Archon?" I said, raising an eyebrow.

He shrugged. "Blame the Greeks. We're stuck with it now."

I laughed. "And who is this Archon?"

His face took on a strange expression. "I don't know."

"You don't know?" I said slowly. "How can you not know?"

"It's a secret, even amongst the group. The heads of each cell have an immense amount of power. For example, they're the only people with access to the full list of Alpha personnel worldwide. If that sort of power fell into the wrong hands, the damage would be catastrophic. So they stay hidden, just in case."

I licked my lips as I tried to process this. "But how does that work?"

"Well, the council has sixteen members, one of whom is in charge. By all appearances, they are just a regular member of the group. Anything that requires their attention as the Archon is dealt with through the Alpha computer network. The commands come anonymously, so nobody but the Archon and their lieutenant know the source."

"Lieutenant?"

He nodded. "The Archon chooses a second in command, someone to take over if anything happens to them. They're like a backup. Otherwise, there would be no way to choose a new leader when the existing one dies. The lieutenant is the only other person that knows who runs the show. It's a little eccentric, I know, but it works."

"I was going to say paranoid, actually."

"Maybe that too. We didn't always do things this way, but about five hundred years ago, one of our enemies managed to infiltrate the group and, through the Archon, they learned everything. We lost hundreds of members and years of progress. So we devised a system to stop that happening again."

It all seemed incredibly mysterious, but then again, that was true of the entire situation. Besides, on some level, that just added to the coolness of it all. I was basically living in a conspiracy theory!

I couldn't help but smile as the full implication of what he'd said sank in. "So, when you said you didn't know, was that you telling the truth, or you toeing the company line?"

"That was me telling you I didn't know," he replied, a twinkle in his eye.

"Right. But if you were in charge, I'm guessing you probably wouldn't tell me anyway, right?"

There was a twinkle in his eye when he replied. "Perhaps not. I need to keep *some* secrets, Sophia."

I sighed dramatically. "I suppose that's fair. Well then, mister councilman, what do we do now?"

I'd intended us to talk a little more about the problems we faced, but apparently he had something else in mind. In response he gently rolled me away from him, then pulling me close until we were spooning. Although I still wore my top, I was naked from the waist down, and the position pressed my bare ass against the growing hardness between his legs. I felt my body stir again.

"Now, we make up for lost time," he replied, his voice growing husky.

And despite the weight of the discussion we'd just had, he quickly convinced me that that was exactly what I wanted to do.

Chapter 7

Sophia

The next few days were a mixture of frustration and joy. By night, I had Sebastian back. We ate together, we talked, and we spent a great deal of time reacquainting ourselves with each other's bodies. Although it hadn't been that long since we'd been intimate, it felt like I was discovering him for the first time all over again.

However, while the sun was up, things were different. As much as we both wanted to just shut ourselves away and ignore everything, the fact was, Sebastian still had a job to do. The threat — whatever it was — wouldn't disappear on its own. If we wanted any hope for some kind of normality in the future, we had to take action.

Or should I say, *he* had to take action. Although he tried to keep me in the loop, my involvement was strictly second hand. There was no way for me to attend their meetings without putting us both at risk. He'd return to his room, which was now our room, and brief me on what had happened that day. They had a few leads, but so far they'd hit nothing but brick walls. Aside from that they apparently spent most of the time fighting about what the next step was.

I tried to amuse myself while he was gone, but it was hard. I wasn't used to being left to my own devices. I hadn't had more than a few days to myself since high school. It didn't help that I was confined to quarters. Until things were safe, Sebastian insisted I did not leave the building. I read a lot and watched more TV than I had in my entire life, but within a few days I felt dangerously close to breaking point. I began having visions of myself as one of those creepy old ladies in Victorian period dramas, who can be seen haunting the windows of ancient manor houses, but never venture out into open air.

Then there was the tension with the group members. Ewan and his cronies continued to make sure I was aware how unwelcome I was. It wasn't outright aggression, but the dark looks and biting remarks told me exactly how they felt.

"Have they said anything about us?" I asked Sebastian, after a particularly bad day.

He frowned and shook his head. "No, actually, they've been strangely silent."

"So that's good, right?"

"I guess," he replied, although he didn't sound convinced.

Most of the others didn't seem to know how to react to me, so they simply ignored my presence. And Joe, the only one I assumed might have talked to me, had gone overseas to attend to some family problem. I felt a little like a ghost, floating unseen and unacknowledged, around that buzzing house.

After several days, my boredom got the better of me and I went in search of a computer. I figured that if I had to kill time, I could at least do it laughing at cats with hilarious facial expressions. Sebastian had a laptop, but he carried it with him during the day. I'd seen a few desktops scattered around the building, and nobody ever seemed to be using them, so I didn't think anyone would mind.

Unfortunately, it wasn't as simple as just sitting down and turning the system on. The PC lit up when I hit the power button, but the screen only got as far as displaying a blinking cursor on a black background, and no amount of resetting or playing with the cables would fix it.

I'd seen Sebastian power up his laptop before, and at some point during the process he always swiped his thumb across the little biometric scanner that hung off the side. This PC had one too, sitting on the desk next to the keyboard. Perhaps the system wouldn't start without the right person in the chair.

Part of me wanted to swipe it myself just to see what would happen. I even got as far as poising my thumb over the pad, but then a voice from the doorway interrupted me.

"I wouldn't do that, if I were you."

I jolted back in my chair. It was Trey. I hadn't seen him since the night I arrived. Apparently he wasn't part of the inner council, so he wasn't holed up here with the rest of them.

"Sorry," I said.

"It's alright. No harm done. You're just lucky I found you when I did. A word of warning, though. Anything that needs a thumbprint you should probably stay away from."

In spite of my embarrassment, my curiosity was now peaked. "Why?"

He smiled. "If you don't have the right authentication, the whole system will shut down until someone comes and checks it out. I figure you could probably do without that attention."

Well, that answered that question. "Right. Thanks for the warning."

He stared at me for a few seconds, and I felt my skin begin

to prickle. It was another of those awkward moments where we were both aware I knew something I shouldn't, but we weren't discussing it. He didn't look concerned at all, but it still made me uncomfortable.

"So, what brings you here anyway? I didn't expect to see you around these parts," I said, trying desperately to fill the silence.

He shrugged and gave a conspiratorial eye roll. "Thomas needed something. You know how it is; the bosses call and we come a-running. Any idea where he is?"

"Actually yeah, I think I saw him chatting to Marcus in the kitchen, before."

Trey's expression darkened a little. Perhaps he and Marcus weren't on the best terms. "Alright, thanks." His smile returned. "Stay out of trouble, hey?"

I gave a little laugh. "I'll do my best."

In spite of how awkward I'd felt, it was nice to have an interaction with Sebastian's colleague that didn't involve any death stares. It made me feel like perhaps there was hope yet on that front.

But, the next day, Sebastian came to me with some news, and that theory promptly went to shit.

"We're leaving," he said.

I rocked back in surprise. "We are? Does that mean it's all over?"

He grimaced. "Unfortunately, no. Several of the council members simply feel like it would be better if you stayed elsewhere until we finish sorting this out." The words came out through gritted teeth. I got the sense it had been another long and bitter argument.

So, I was being exiled. On one hand, it was actually a bit of a relief. I was sick of being trapped here, constantly feeling like the awkward relative nobody actually wants around. But, on the other hand, the danger outside these walls was very real.

"I thought it wasn't safe out there," I said carefully.

He sighed. "It's not. But don't worry, they're not sending you home. I talked them into a compromise. This isn't the only secure facility Alpha owns. We've got several other places, scattered around the city, so we're going to move to one of the empty ones. It won't be as heavily guarded as this place, but it has all the same security measures. We'll be just as safe as we are now."

"Okay," I said, although there was a slight tremble in my voice. What other response could I give? There didn't seem to be any point arguing.

He gazed at me for a few seconds before lowering himself onto the bed next to me and taking my hand in his. "Hey, it'll be okay. Trust me. I'm coming too, and I'd die before I let anything happen to you."

I nodded. "I know. I just hate feeling so damn powerless, you know? I'm just a pawn, being shuffled around the board; only it's not a game, it's my bloody life."

"I know," he replied, offering me a sad little smile. "I know."

The next day, we left. There was no fanfare. Nobody even said goodbye. I guess that was to be expected.

We were met outside by two hulking rent-a-suits, who Sebastian introduced as Tony and Aaron. They were apparently going to be our daytime security team.

He was coming with me now to help me settle in, but he'd have to commute back to the main house every day to continue working on the crisis.

After about thirty minutes, we pulled up in front of a small but modern looking house on a quiet, leafy street. At first glance it appeared utterly normal, but the biometric scanner on the front door and the bars over the windows hinted that this was something more than an average residence.

"They're bulletproof," he said, following my gaze. "The doors too." Reaching out, he thumbed the touch pad by the front door, and the lock clicked open. "Nobody is getting in here without the proper authorisation. And to even try, they have to deal with Tony and Aaron first. The whole house will be under round the clock surveillance."

Some of the tension I'd been carrying around inside me dissipated. The place certainly seemed as secure as he'd claimed.

The two guards stationed themselves outside, leaving the entire house to Sebastian and I. It was nice to finally feel like we had our own space again. Despite its size, the main house had, at times, felt cramped, and the pervasive air of concern and hostility had made it a less than pleasant living environment.

Sebastian produced some takeaway food from somewhere and we ate it sprawled out in front of the television, mocking the terribleness of the reality shows that seemed to dominate every network. It wasn't a particularly interesting evening by most standards, but I found myself laughing harder than I had in weeks. Leaving the Alpha headquarters had lifted a weight from my shoulders that I hadn't even realised I was carrying.

After dinner, Sebastian disappeared into the back of the house for a minute and returned carrying a box.

"I have something for you," he said, his tone once again serious.

"Oh?"

He opened the container to reveal a petite silver gun. My breath caught in my throat. "I want you to have this," he said, removing it and holding it out to me.

"Sebastian, I don't know the first thing about guns." Just the idea of having something so deadly in my hands filled me with an uneasy energy.

"I know. I'm not expecting you to go take out our enemies all by yourself. In truth, I doubt that you'll ever have to use it. I meant what I said about this place being secure. This is just a precaution, nothing more." He reached out with his free hand and cupped my chin, his thumb grazing my cheek with the utmost tenderness. "I can't be with you all the time, and the thought of not being here to protect you myself... please, it would make me feel better."

The concern in his eyes was enough to allay my hesitation. Gingerly, I reached out and took the weapon from him. It's cliché, but it was surprisingly heavy. The metal felt cold against my skin.

"This is the safety," he said, indicating near the trigger. "Don't switch that off unless you mean it. The gun carries thirteen rounds and is already loaded."

Closing my hands more tightly around the grip, I raised it slowly in front of me. I didn't have any illusions about my ability to actually hit anything, but I did feel a certain sense of comfort with that weight between my fingers.

"Okay." Holding death in my hand, I suddenly felt the need to make a joke. "You know, I'm pretty sure none of my friend's partners have ever given them a lethal weapon before. I'm surely the luckiest girl in the whole world."

The tension eased on his face. "I'm glad I could be your first."

"So, what else is there to do around this place?" I asked, setting the weapon aside. "You know, besides play with my new firearm."

"Not a whole lot." He grinned wickedly and slid closer, looping his hands under my legs and lifting them over his lap until I lay cradled in his arms. "Although I have a few ideas about how we can take advantage of our newfound privacy."

"Oh? And what might those be?" I replied as sweetly as possible.

He leaned in to brush a soft kiss across my cheek. "Well, I thought perhaps I'd see how many different rooms I could fuck you in."

"I think I'd like that very much," I replied, already feeling my pulse quicken.

Suffice it to say that there were no rooms left unchristened by the time we finally collapsed into bed.

Chapter 8

Sophia

For a little while, the novelty of being somewhere fresh buoyed my mood. I explored the new house, and spent many hours pottering around with a glass of wine and a book. But soon enough, my frustration returned. Each morning, Sebastian would kiss me on the head and then disappear through the bedroom door, not returning until well after sundown. In many ways, he had little more freedom than me, but at least he had a mission. I, on the other hand, was left to simply float around, entirely without purpose.

I tried engaging the security guards in a little banter, but it quickly became apparently that all of the steroids must have burned their fun glands into oblivion. They were about as friendly as a pair of rocks, and even less interesting; I quickly abandoned all hope of alleviating my boredom through conversation.

At my request, Sebastian had brought me a laptop, so I turned to surfing job hunting websites online. I knew it was masochistic to taunt myself like that, but I couldn't help it.

After a decade of thinking about nothing but my career, I couldn't just switch off that part of my brain. To be honest, I wasn't sure there were many other parts anymore. It turned out there were several positions going at top tier firms, including one at Little Bell's biggest rival. Any one of them would have been perfect for me, and I knew I stood a good chance if I decided to apply.

I stared at the screen for a while, before closing the laptop and setting it purposefully aside. *Well, there you go. Who knows, maybe they'll still be available in a few weeks and all this will have blown over.*

But as I lay in bed that night, I couldn't stop thinking about what I'd found. Getting back to work was exactly what I needed. With all day to myself, I couldn't help but dwell on my situation. Being unemployed and trapped in a house, with mysterious forces plotting God knows what all around me, was hardly a recipe for inner peace.

"You know, I'm going a little crazy here," I said the next day, when we were sitting in the lounge room after dinner.

He shot me a sympathetic look. "I know it's rough. Hopefully we'll have something soon. In the meantime, try to relax and enjoy the time off."

"Have you seen me try to relax?" I replied. "It's a train wreck. Yesterday I actually rearranged every book in the study by author name, just to feel like I'd actually achieved something for the day."

He laughed.

"Incidentally, you have an awful lot of cook books from the fifties in there. Anyway, relaxation isn't my M.O," I continued. "I need to be out there, getting my life back on track. The longer I wait to find another job, the harder it's going to be. I get that the situation is dangerous, but I want something to come back to when it's all over."

He stared at me for several seconds, a strange smile playing on his lips.

"What?" I asked, realising that something wasn't right. He shouldn't have been smiling.

He opened his mouth, then closed it again, before standing up and walking over to his desk. "I was going to wait until after all of this was sorted out, but I guess there's no harm in showing you now."

"Showing me what?" I asked, feeling a rush of excitement.

He returned holding a small stack of paper.

"This," he said. "I know you have a thing about people helping you, but hopefully you can make an exception in this case."

With some trepidation I began to read, but before I'd made it more than half a page I found myself grinning like an idiot. "Oh my God," I said. "Where did you get these?"

"A friend of a friend," he replied nonchalantly.

"Well your friend struck gold," I said, flipping through several more pages. "My God, the partners are going to flip when they see this."

In my hands, I held a printout of a chain of emails that stretched back over several years. Sebastian and I were no strangers to a bit of written flirtation, but these took the idea of sexting to a whole new level. We're talking bad eighties porno script, and judging by the phrasing, it was just a prelude to what the couple were actually doing in the bedroom.

The email addresses weren't instantly familiar — they looked like personal accounts — but the signatures were.

Alan Beatie and Jennifer Smart.

"I thought you'd be pleased," Sebastian replied.

That was the understatement of the century. A long term relationship between an associate and her superior was already enough to land them in serious trouble, but this went a step further. Interspersed between the racier messages were numerous requests for favours and plenty of signs of preferential treatment. Judging by the dates, their arrangement had started before Jennifer was even promoted. It didn't take a genius to see how the other partners would view that. It felt like Christmas come early.

And then I spotted the coup de grace. "Holy shit." I held up one specific line for him to read. "Did you see this?"

He grinned and nodded.

Thank you for finally dealing with that little bitch Sophia. I'm sure I can think of a few creative ways to reward you ;)

It was morbidly gratifying to finally see her talk about me the way I always suspected she did. The prim, sweet girl that roamed our office building was nowhere in sight, here. These emails were Jennifer unfiltered, and it showed exactly what a nasty piece of work she really was. Although my name came up most frequently, she seemed to have a grudge against almost everyone who posed even a vague threat to her advancement up the ladder. For a brief moment, I actually felt bad for her, for being so insecure, but that was quickly crushed under a torrent of glorious satisfaction at knowing she was finally going to get what she deserved.

"I knew they couldn't have had a decent reason for firing you."

I nodded, still mesmerised by the words in front of me. "You think it'll be enough to get my job back?"

"Definitely. These make it pretty clear that there was more to your dismissal than the quality of your work."

I realised I was grinning like an idiot. "I'll go first thing tomorrow," I said, already playing the confrontation through in my head.

His expression dropped a fraction. "I'd rather you wait until we've dealt with our other problem. It's still dangerous out there."

For a second, I thought I'd misheard. "You seriously expect me to sit on this? Why give it to me at all?"

He shrugged uncomfortably. "You seemed upset. I thought it might make you feel better knowing you can wander back into Little Bell when this is all over."

"And what am I meant to do in the meantime? Keep twiddling my thumbs around here? Look, I'm not downplaying the risk. I know it's not safe, but the truth is, we have no idea how long this is going to take. Sure, it could be a week, but it could be a month, or two, or six. Who's to say they're even going to show their faces again, without an opportunity?" I closed my eyes briefly, trying to rein in my emotions. I felt like a hormonal teenage girl again, flitting from jubilant to angry to upset in the blink of an eye. "I need *something* Sebastian. Being stuck here is killing me — pardon the pun. Surely we can find a way to make it work? You go to and from work every day and you're still in one piece."

His jaw tightened and he glanced away. "That's true." He pondered for a while. "I'm sorry." Sliding closer, he pulled me against him and leaned down to kiss my hair. "I just find the idea of leaving you exposed terrifying. But you're right, this isn't fair on you. How about this: you go in there tomorrow and kick some ass, and once you have your job back, Aaron and Tony will take you to and from the office every day. As long as you don't leave the building, you'll be fine. Several thousand witnesses should be enough to deter anyone from trying anything."

I found myself grinning once more. "Not to mention building security. You, sir, have a deal." Snuggling in against his chest, I began reading over the emails again. "God, I can't wait to see her smarmy little face."

* * * * *

"Hello, Jennifer," I said in my sweetest voice, as I peeked my head around her door.

For a brief second, shock registered on her face, although it was gone in an instant. "Sophia. What a pleasant surprise. I thought you were still on leave."

"I was. I just dropped in to deliver something to Mr Bell."

Her brow furrowed. I think she could tell by my demeanour that something wasn't quite right, but she didn't know what. "That seems... unorthodox."

"Oh, I know. I wouldn't have bothered him, except I recently came into possession of some information that I knew he'd want to see."

"Oh?" She sounded uncomfortable, which only made my smile grow. I knew it was petty and childish, but it felt indescribably satisfying to finally be able to toy with her as she had so many times with me.

"Yeah. It's a bit of a scandal, actually." I leaned in close, as though sharing a secret with a friend. "Apparently, one of the partners has been fooling around with a senior associate. I got a look at the emails they've been sending each other. Some of the things they've been writing... well, graphic doesn't even began to describe them. But the worst part? He's been doing her all kinds of favours around the office. He even gave her a promotion after a weekend away together. Pretty shocking, right? You think your work is what's important, and then you hear about something like this. It's enough to make you sick."

The expression on her face was priceless. Her eyes were open so wide I thought they might pop out of her head, and her mouth worked soundlessly, as though she might somehow still be able to argue her way out of the situation. She looked like one of those rotating carnival clowns.

For a few seconds I simply stood and enjoyed. "Anyway, as you can imagine, Mr Bell is taking the matter very seriously. The partner is in with him right now I believe, and he should be calling the associate any moment. I can't imagine either of them have much longer with the company."

In a piece of spectacularly fortunate timing, at that exact moment, Jennifer's phone began to ring.

"Oh, you have a call," I said. "I'll let you go, then. Just wanted to share the news. Have a nice day."

I don't know how I did it, but I managed to turn around and leave without letting out a cheer, although internally I was giving myself a million high fives. Even Jennifer herself would have been proud of that performance. It had been as chirpy and fake as any act of hers.

I could have been the bigger woman and let that be the end of it, but after years of torture, the moral high ground was the last thing on my mind. This was my moment and I was going to enjoy the hell out of it. After a brief visit to see what had become of my office, I hunted Elle down and dragged her out into the main foyer to wait with me.

"Oh. My. God," she said, when I relayed what had happened. "You're my fucking hero. What did she say when you told her?"

"Nothing. She just sat there growing redder and redder, like someone was pumping her full of hot air."

She laughed. "Christ, I wish I'd been there to see it. That must have been the most satisfying thing in the world."

"It was pretty amazing," I replied.

"How the hell did you get access to her email, anyway?"

I shrugged. "I didn't. Some mysterious little bird forwarded them to me."

"You're kidding, right?"

I shook my head. It was a pretty flimsy lie, but ironically it was more believable than the truth. *Oh, yeah, my boyfriend is part of a secret society that hacked Jennifer's email.* That would go down a treat. "They just showed up in my inbox the other day."

She shook her head in disbelief. "Well, apparently you have a fairy godmother looking out for you."

I couldn't help but grin at the Cinderella reference. "You know, maybe I do."

At that moment, Jennifer appeared around the corner, escorted by building security. She was the picture of a sudden firing; eyes blank, skin deathly white, possessions clutched listlessly in a cardboard box against her chest. There had been no dancing around the issue with her, no feints involving temporary leave to ease the blow. She'd been summarily let go, and company policy dictated that she had to leave immediately. There was too much sensitive information at stake to allow ex-employees to linger.

She did her best to maintain the veneer of superiority, although the smeared mascara running below her eyes certainly detracted from the effect, and the moment she saw me her expression crumpled. I'd positioned myself perfectly, exactly where she'd stood during my walk of shame. There was nothing sweet about my smile this time. I let loose with everything I had. I even threw in my most sarcastic wave for good measure.

Elle was a little more direct. "Seeya, bitch," she said, as they swept past and into the lift. Jennifer flinched as if struck.

As the doors closed, Elle drew a deep breath and smiled. "Is it just me, or does the air smell a little sweeter in here all of a sudden?"

I sniffed pointedly. "You know, I think it does. Must be

the lack of bullshit."

She laughed. "So, please tell me this means you're coming back? This place is a bore without you."

"It will likely be a bore either way. But yeah, I'm back. Apparently they were getting ready to make my leave more permanent this week, so the timing is perfect. I'm still on the books, so we don't even have to do any paperwork."

Elle clapped. "Awesome. Surely this calls for a celebration?"

I winced, remembering Sebastian's rules. As appealing as an old-school office bender sounded, it wasn't safe. "Let me settle back in and then we'll talk. Okay?"

She looked a little disappointed, but didn't question. "Sure. Well, thanks for inviting me to the show, but I should get back to it. Wrights won't prosecute itself."

"No problem. Seeya round."

Once she'd disappeared around the corner, I took a moment just soaking in my surroundings. That might seem like a strange thing to do — I mean, for all its prestige, it was really just an office — but after having given the bulk of the last six years to Little Bell, sometimes it felt more like home than my own house. When Sebastian had handed me those pages, I'd been fairly confident it would be enough to get me back in the door, but I hadn't been certain until now. I was back. At least one part of the nightmare was over.

It didn't take me long to find my feet again. After letting everyone know I was available again, work quickly began to flow in. In just a few hours, I was once again neck deep in case files. Ordinarily that might have had me slightly frazzled, but today, I couldn't wipe the smile off my face.

Surprisingly, Sebastian was waiting for me when we got back. Most days he didn't return until well after dinner.

"I wanted to be here when you got back from your first

day," he said when I asked. He held a bottle of champagne in his hands, and there were two glasses laid out on the bench in front of him.

"Aww, that's very sweet of you," I said, leaning in for a lingering kiss. "But you didn't have to go to all this trouble. It's not like I got a new job. It's the same one I always had."

"That doesn't make it any less worth celebrating." He gave a wolfish grin. "Besides, I felt like champagne."

I laughed. "Ah, now the truth comes out."

He poured and then we settled into the couch.

"So, how was it? Everything went well?"

"You could say that. Evil was vanquished, order restored and all that good stuff."

"I'm glad to hear it. It must feel nice to be back."

I nodded. "Hell yes it does. I can honestly say, I don't think I've ever been so happy to be so busy in my life."

"I'm glad."

"Ernest also dropped a few not so subtle hints about 'recently vacated positions' that might need to be filled."

His face lit up and he pulled me in for a hug. "Congratulations! That's wonderful."

"It is, isn't it?"

"I bet you'd have been promoted years ago if not for those two," he said. "You'll be running that place one day, mark my words."

"Yeah, then maybe I'll have the credentials to join Alpha myself."

He gave a wry shake of his head. "You'd seriously want to do that, having seen what you've seen?"

"I don't know. It's not like it hasn't entered my mind. If you ignore all the guns and kidnappings and such, it is pretty cool." I took a sip of champagne. "Besides, it would certainly solve one of our current predicaments."

"I suppose it would."

"How exactly does one join anyway? Joe said he kind of just plucked you out of the army."

His smile gained a hint of nostalgia. "He told you about that, hey? Yeah, I'm not sure what I would have done if he hadn't found me. I was pretty lost, up until that point. Now I've actually got a purpose.

"As for recruitment, there's no one way. You get people like Thomas, who just work ridiculously hard in their chosen field until we can't help but notice them. He made an absolute killing working for one of the big oil companies, before we found him. And then you've got the guys like Trey, who just get in on their family name."

"Ooh, trust fund baby, is he? I had no idea. He doesn't seem like *that* much of a dick."

Sebastian laughed. "He's fine, most of the time, although to be honest, a bunch of us didn't want to accept his application. We like to recruit people on their merits, not their bloodline, but his dad was a member before him, and he desperately wanted his son to follow in his footsteps. I think it was one of those old money tradition things. Anyway, he pulled some strings and had enough friends that eventually he got his way. Keep that to yourself, though."

"Yeah, sure. I guess since my family has all the eminence of a McNugget Happy Meal, I'll have to go the hard working route."

His expression lost a little of its playfulness. "Let's cross that bridge if we get there, hey?"

I wasn't really sure if I was being serious, but the idea seemed to distress him, so I decided to drop it.

The next few days took on a strangely comfortable quality. If you ignored the nightmarish backdrop, Sebastian and I almost looked like an ordinary, wholesome, professional couple. Each day we'd race through a quick breakfast together before heading to our respective offices. We'd slave away for ten hours or so, occasionally calling each other to whisper sweet nothings, before returning home and spending a few hours in front of the TV or making love, and then collapsing into bed and doing it all again. I'd never really pictured myself being in a long term relationship, but if I had, that was basically how it would have gone. Only the occasional harried expression on Sebastian's face and the presence of our little security team managed to shatter the illusion of normality.

Of course, things were far from fixed. Work was a welcome distraction, but it didn't quite temper the edginess that I seemed to carry around with me permanently, now. In fact, if anything, it made it worse. Logically, I knew that nothing was likely to happen. My building was swarming with people until well past dinner time every night, and my bodyguards met me just feet from the front door. Someone would have to be incredibly bold or incredibly stupid to try anything there. But, nonetheless, I couldn't shake the sensation that I was constantly being watched. It made me jumpy and agitated.

Sebastian seemed to recognise that I was struggling, because he was really putting in a ton of effort. Between the sexy texts and cute little gifts he had delivered to my office — I'm not afraid to admit that I'm a sucker for a bunch of red roses — I was actually feeling rather spoilt. And then he delivered the coup de grace.

On Saturday, I arrived at home to find a note on the kitchen counter. Despite the fact that there was nobody else living there, he'd addressed it like all the others. *Sophia.* Unlike his last letter, this one sent a wave of excitement shooting though me. He was back to his old tricks.

With eager fingers, I unfolded it.

Dear Sophia.

I may be a little later than normal tonight. Hopefully you can excuse me. I know things have been a little difficult lately, so I've decided we need a nice romantic night together. I'd like you to set up a few things for me before I get home.

In the freezer you'll find a bag of ice. Take it into the bedroom and fill the bucket that's on the dresser. There's a bottle of champagne next to it which I'd like you to chill.

In the bedroom you'll also find a box of matches and several candles. There's nothing like a little mood lighting. Light them and scatter them around the room.

Finally, on the bed is an item I believe you will remember fondly. After you've removed everything else you're wearing, put it on and then wait for me on the bed lying face down.

I'll see you soon.

-S

I found myself biting my lip as I read, my skin already prickling with heat. The scene he described was basically the epitome of romance, but the heavy, commanding tone with which he wrote was unmistakable. There was more afoot here than was immediately obvious. It had been a while since one of his letters, long enough to make me heady with anticipation.

After ducking quickly to the freezer, I made a beeline for the bedroom, already suspecting that I knew what I'd find. I wasn't let down. If I'd had any doubts that tonight would be kinkier than our recent sessions, they vanished the moment my eyes fell on the bed. Lying on the quilt was the blindfold Sebastian had originally left for me in the hotel several months ago. Just thinking about that night sent something warm surging between my legs. The sting of his hand, the bite of the rope; that had been the night when everything changed. I'd gone in one woman and come out another.

Placing the champagne inside the bucket I buried it in ice, then lit the candles and dimmed the light. I had to admit, the scene did look incredibly romantic. After stripping, I knelt on the bed and wrapped the black silk around my head, knotting it firmly at the back. Last time I'd been hesitant, even a little frightened, but now could barely contain my excitement. Sebastian had taught me well the pleasure of sensory deprivation.

For a while I lay, enjoying the silence as anticipation rose inside me. I knew the wait was part of the experience. My wandering mind was winding me up as effectively as any foreplay. Would it be another spanking? More restraint? Or did he have other tricks up his sleeve?

It could have been fifteen minutes or an hour, I'm not sure, but eventually, I heard the tell-tale click of the front door unlocking. My body tensed. I assumed he'd come straight to me, but everything remained silent. I realised I'd left the bedroom door open and the floors here were carpeted, meaning I'd have no indication when he finally arrived. He could have been in the room at that very moment.

I squirmed a little, as some strange amalgamation of discomfort and desire lodged itself in my stomach. That was one of my favourite parts of discovering my submissive side; the realisation that other emotions besides arousal could be a turn on too. I felt more in tune with myself than ever before.

It doesn't matter if he's here yet or not. He told me to wait, and so wait I will. He'll come when he's ready.

I held my position.

Chapter 9

Sebastian

She flinched a little when I entered, although I hadn't made a sound. Perhaps some subtle shift in the air had given me away. Or perhaps she simply knew me too well. Regardless, she continued to lie still and silent.

I had no idea how she'd become such an amazing sub in such a short time. We hadn't delved into anything too kinky for a while, but seeing her like that made me desperate to do it more. There's something so erotic about coming home to a girl presenting herself for you, exactly as you instructed. She'd followed my directions to the letter: the champagne was chilling, the candles were lit, and the blindfold was in place.

I spent a few moments just taking in the sight of her. She was absolutely stunning; her hair was splayed out across her back like a chestnut river, her creamy skin bathed in candle light. I'd never seen a woman with a more gorgeous figure; perfectly proportioned curves but not an ounce more fat than necessary. Just being near her naked body had my blood rushing in my veins.

She didn't even jump when I spoke. "Well, isn't this romantic."

She gave a little laugh. "Is it? You'll have to fill me in. I'm having a little trouble seeing right now." It was funny, although my comment had been fairly innocuous, there was something different about her voice. It was softer, more compliant. The change occurred whenever we made love, whether there was kink involved or not. I don't even think she realised it was happening, as though she simply slipped from one persona to the other, automatically. I was amazed she'd never realised her predilection before. She was a natural.

I walked over and dragged a hand gently down her back. So soft, like stroking silk. She trembled a little, but otherwise didn't move.

"I have something special planned tonight," I said. "Something new."

"I suspected as much," she replied. "I don't suppose you're going to tell me what it is, though?"

I chuckled. "Now where would be the fun in that?"

I moved over to the dresser and withdrew a bottle I'd stashed there earlier. "Have I told you how gorgeous you are today?" I asked.

Her lips quirked up. "Not in at least ten hours."

"Then I have been remiss," I replied, moving closer. "I have to admit, I've been thinking about this all day. I could barely wait to get my hands on this body again."

"Your hands have been on this body a lot lately."

I slipped onto the bed and straddled her legs. "Not like this," I replied, popping the cap and squeezing a large drop of massage oil onto her back.

She twitched and let out a little noise of surprise, but it quickly morphed into a groan as my hands began to work across her skin. "God, a girl could get used to this after work."

She wasn't the only one enjoying herself. The sight of her skin, slick and shining, was like a shot of testosterone straight to my veins, and she felt magnificent between my fingers. I kneaded my way slowly up and down her back, paying attention to each individual muscle. In my younger days, in a spontaneous attempt to impress a woman, I'd taken a massage class, and while I was a little rusty, with a little trial and error I found the sort of pressure and pace Sophia liked. More than a few areas felt tight, so I spent extra time on them, enjoying the sensation of her gradually melting beneath me.

The lower I moved down her body, the deeper her noises became, the mood gradually shifting from sensual to sexual. Applying more oil I began working the firm globes of her ass slowly, occasionally dipping close to her sex but taking pains not to actually make contact. She shifted, letting out several little whimpers, but didn't voice any objection. Seeing that restraint got me so ridiculously hard. Only a month ago, she'd already be begging for me to touch her there. She'd beg eventually, I'd make sure of it, but the fact that she held back now showed how far her self-control had come.

I had no doubt that she knew there was more to the evening than a simple massage — we'd been together long enough for my surprises to be truly unexpected anymore — but I was still looking forward to what came next. I love that sense of unpredictability, of taking my partner into unknown territory. The uncertainty of it heightens everything. I could almost feel the anticipation vibrating through her body.

"You have magic hands," she said, when I finally pulled them away.

"I'm glad you enjoyed the warm up."

She paused. "Warm up for what?" Her voice was breathy, with the barest current of trepidation flowing through it. So fucking sexy.

Rather than answer, I leaned across to the side table and scooped up one of the candles. "Do you trust me?" I asked.

There was no hesitation this time. "Yes." After everything that had happened in the last few weeks, it was amazing to hear such certainty. I had no idea where she found the strength to forgive me, let alone trust me again. That trust was the most important thing in the world to me now, and I'd die before I breached it again.

"Good. I want you to extend your arms and press your palms against the headboard. I'm not going to bind you this time. It will be up to you to restrain yourself. If your hands move before I say so, there will be consequences. Understand?"

She nodded.

"Okay, this will be hot."

And before she had a chance to speak, I tilted the candle slightly, sending a small glob of wax tumbling onto the small of her back. Her body arched and she let out a short cry.

"Too hot?" I asked.

She assessed for a few seconds. "No, just unexpected." She let out a little laugh. "Is that wax?"

"Yes."

"I was wracking my brains trying to work out what you might do, but I didn't even consider the candles."

I grinned. "That was the plan."

"Well, it feels good," she said, as I poured again. Gradually, I worked my way across her body, varying the height and size of the drops to create different temperatures. There was something so artful about the act of covering her like that, the redness of the wax in stark contrast to the whiteness of her flesh. And the way she reacted, the little sighs and tremors that passed through her as the liquid hardened against her skin, had me aroused nearly to the point of pain. At the angle she was lying, I could see the lips of her pussy, nestled tantalisingly between those perfect cheeks, and in my head I was already playing through what it would be like when I was finally inside her. That divine warmth and maddening softness, the way her body would tremble and her voice would break as I took her, forcing her towards climax.

I began using my free hand to shape the wax, dragging my fingers through it, enjoying the heat and the sensation of her skin. She seemed to like that a lot. Soon, the whole bottom half of her back was a vibrant haphazard crosshatching of crimson.

"You must be making quite a mess back there," she said.

"You look beautiful," I replied. "But we're just getting started."

Setting the candle down and climbing free of her, I stepped over to the dresser and scooped up the champagne holder. Now that she was clued in to the game, she understood almost immediately.

"Oh god," she said, as I straddled her once more. Leaning down, I brushed a kiss softly against the back of her neck while reaching into the bucket.

"Now this, this will be cold."

She was trembling before I even touched her, but that first moment was like electricity, her body convulsing as I pressed the ice cube against her. Watching intensely for any sign of real discomfort, I began to trace the cube down her spine. She continued to wriggle, her breath hitching, but the noises slipping from her mouth were those of pleasure. Being a dom is always a bit like walking a tight rope; you're constantly pushing your partner's limits, trying new things, and it can be incredibly easy to accidentally slip across the murky line between enjoyment and genuine distress. Temperature play, in particular, is a sensitive activity, but Sophia appeared to be loving it.

The ice melted quickly, her body still radiating residual heat, so I took another piece and repeated the path, this time trailing my tongue behind on her chilled skin.

She let out a long sigh.

"You like that?"

She nodded. "The contrast is amazing. Keep going."

And so I did, slowly traversing the still clean portions of her body, savouring the taste of her, the texture of her skin, the feminine scent that filled my nostrils until she dominated my senses.

"Let's try both together," I said.

Her sounds grew louder as I began to alternate hot and cold, stroking with ice then chasing with wax. When the cube was nearly melted down I let it sit in place and tipped the candle directly over it, sending a stream of icy water swirled with crimson heat flowing down her side.

Now that she was in the zone, it was time for the main event. Stashing the candle again I took another cube, this time focusing on her ass. Slowly I circled each cheek, making no effort to ease the chill. The skin down there is more sensitive, and she shivered and twitched at my touch. Soon her entire ass was slick and goose pimpled.

"Should I go lower?" I asked.

"Yes," she breathed.

She inhaled sharply as I slipped my hand between her cheeks, rolling the tiny nub of ice softly around the puckered rosette inside.

"Jesus Christ."

"I still want to fuck you here you know," I said, slipping one chilled finger just half an inch inside her, drawing a short gasp from her lips. "Maybe tonight?" I left the question hanging in the air. I already knew it wouldn't be now. I'd have her there eventually — I intended to have all of her, everything she could give — but not tonight. Of course, that didn't mean I couldn't plant the seed, make her wonder.

I slipped the ice lower still. Parting her legs, I stroked it gently across her inner thighs, gradually working my way towards her pussy. She was incredibly turned on by this point. The scent of her excitement filled the air, and her lips were glistening despite the fact that I'd yet to use the ice there. I desperately wanted to slip my finger into that softness, to bury my tongue in it and lick her until she couldn't even speak, but I restrained myself. I found the act of forcing self-control extremely exciting. Waiting now meant more pleasure for both of us later. That said, I'd never found waiting so difficult as when I had her in front of me.

Every time my hand drifted closer to her sex, her hips bucked a little more wildly.

"Do you want me to touch you?" I asked.

"Yes," she replied, no longer making any effort to disguise the desire in her voice.

"You'll have to do better than that."

"Please, Sebastian, please touch my clit."

I poised my hand above the entrance to her sex, my fingers splayed around it, the ice pressed just above her entrance. I love the rush of power I feel at moments like that. For me, kink has never been about the pain or the taboo, it's about power and intimacy. This beautiful woman had given herself over to me. She'd put her pleasure entirely in my hands. Nothing is more intimate than that.

"You *have* done very well," I said, brushing the ice ever so gently along her slit. "But there's one more thing I want to do first."

She let out a groan of disappointment, but it quickly cut off as I began cupping and kneading her ass. God, it was so firm, so perfect. I could have played with just that part of her for hours. But I didn't want to lose the effect of what I'd just done. Her skin was still icy and wet, and it made a delicious cracking noise as I slapped my palm gently against it.

Instantly her body tensed. She knew what that symbolised, and although I'd spanked her once before, it was some time ago. I didn't blame her for being a little fearful.

"But I kept my hands exactly where you told me to!" she said.

I laughed. There was still plenty of vanilla in her. "I know. This isn't a punishment. It's a reward." I leaned in close, stroking her skin tenderly. "Remember how much you enjoyed being spanked last time? Remember how wet it made you?"

She swallowed loudly, her cheeks flushing pink, but after a few seconds she nodded.

"Good. You can lift up your hands now and get onto your knees."

She did as I asked, the smallest tremor evident in her movements. Sliding in next to her, I wrapped my hands around her hips and lifted her over my lap until she lay, bent over my knees, across the bed.

I took a moment to admire her in that position. I could feel the heat of her arousal radiating onto my thigh. She was so sexy and so strong, yet she allowed herself to be so vulnerable. It was one of the most erotic things I'd ever seen. "Wonderful. Are you ready?"

She drew a long breath, then nodded.

"Say it."

"I'm ready to be spanked." It was barely more than a whisper.

Those words were music to my ears. "Okay."

And without further ado, I pulled my hand away and

brought it whipping back against her left cheek. The crack was much louder this time, ringing throughout the room. She bit back a cry.

"It will sting more this time because of the cold," I told her, pausing to admire the small red circle that was blooming on her skin. "That's part of the fun of temperature play, it sets all your nerves into overdrive."

I started softly, easing her into it, alternating from side to side and soothing each cheek with a gentle rub before continuing. I kept my pace uneven, never pausing the same amount of times between blows, never allowing her to develop a rhythm. With the blindfold on, she was constantly guessing.

Her body flinched with every blow, her breath coming short and sharp, but the pitch of her cries and the quirk of her mouth told me all I needed to know.

"Are you enjoying that?" I asked, landing a slightly harder slap.

"Yes," she replied, her voice thick with lust.

"Shall I smack you harder?"

She nodded quickly, now utterly shameless.

My next blow was stronger, and she yelped as it landed, driving her crotch into my leg and sending a pulse of pleasure shooting through my own body as she pressed against my cock.

I sped up, losing myself in the moment. With every blow she grew more excited, and that in turn stoked my own arousal. There's something intoxicating about the connection I feel during a scene like that. The trust, the sensuality, the vortex of sensations; it's a potent cocktail.

Soon, her entire ass was rosy and glowing. I paused, parting her cheeks with my hand, mesmerised by the wetness between. Unable to resist, I punctuated my next smack by slipping a finger from my free hand inside her. She let out a

97

long moan, a sound of pure animal pleasure, as all her muscles clenched tight around me.

"Christ, look how turned on you are," I said.

She writhed beneath me as I explored her, revelling in the way her body hummed as I stroked her G-spot. I'd been with a lot of other women, but none looked so perfectly alluring in their pleasure as she did. Something about her just sent all of my blood rushing south.

Slipping my finger free, I left it poised against her entrance, and then smacked her again. "Do you think I should keep going?"

"Please," she replied, sounding almost pained.

Stroking the outside of her sex softly, I leaned down close to her head, planting a slow kiss below her ear, letting her answer hang in the air just long enough to make her unsure.

Then, when the quick little breaths falling from her lips reached fever pitch, I whispered in her ear, "Okay," and plunged back in. Her whole body stiffened as I found that soft pad once more, savouring the way each tiny touch echoed through her. At the same time, I resumed spanking, trying to weave that pain in time with her pleasure.

The combination was nearly too much for her. In less than a minute her cries reached their crescendo.

"Are you ready to come for me?" I asked her.

"Oh God, yes!"

"Then do it."

And a few seconds later, her whole body stiffened. The sight of her, those trembling muscles and that perfectly flushed skin, was nearly enough to make me come too. I never tired of doing that to her. I could have watched her come all day.

When the room was finally quiet again, save for her little sighs of satisfaction, I lifted her off my knees and onto the bed and reached for my belt. The time for restraint was over.

In a matter of seconds I was naked and straddling her prone form. She said nothing, simply arching her ass up towards me and propping herself up on her elbows. So perfectly ready and willing. I paused a moment, to take her in, stroking my cock back and forward between her cheeks. The vibrant red of her skin had dulled now to a soft glow, although she still flinched a little at my touch.

A long moan escaped my lips as I pushed my way into her, her body welcoming me with a familiarity that set all my nerves tingling. She was incredibly wet from our games before, and I was able to bury most of my length in a single stroke.

"I swear you get bigger every time," she said, her voice low.

I responded by seizing her hips and pushing myself in further still, until I was pressed up against her. I started slow, giving her time to adjust, relishing her slickness and warmth. Our bodies quickly fell into sync, hers bucking gently beneath me, pressing upwards in time with my rhythm. Each stroke was almost torturous. Nothing had ever felt as good as she did.

Soon, that exquisite softness became too much. I longed to let go.

"Put your arms behind your back," I said.

She did as I'd asked, resting her head on the pillow in front. Somehow, that position made her look even hotter, the subtle angle of her back making her ass look good enough to eat. Crossing her wrists and pinning them behind her with one hand, I began to fuck her harder, using her arms as leverage to drive her against me. Her body was completely mine now, and the volume of her cries instantly increased. There was no doubt she loved being rendered so powerless as much as I loved rendering her so.

The wax on her back had hardened, and with every punishing thrust, little flakes broke off and drifted down onto the bed. I forced myself into her with a single minded urgency, as though by pushing deeper I could claim just a little more of her. There was nothing else in the world at that moment but her body beneath mine.

Her muscles tightened and her sounds became choked, and then another orgasm ripped through her. Then sensation of having her come around my cock drove me wild. I could feel every trembling contraction vibrate through her and into me.

It was too much. I felt the vestiges of my self-control shatter along with her. A mounting tension began building inside me as my hips took on a life of their own. It started low in my balls, radiating upwards and through my shaft then spiralling out further still.

"I'm going to come on you, Sophia," I panted, savouring the little sounds of encouragement the spilt from her lips.

As my pleasure reached its apex, I pulled myself free. There was a bursting sensation and my vision dimmed as I spurted liquid heat onto her back. Seeing her like that, coated in wax and water and me, was the perfect conclusion to the night's activities. It was so fucking hot seeing her marked in that way.

"Well now I *know* you've made a mess back there," she said.

I laughed. "I may have. Let me fix that." I went to get a towel and took my time wiping her clean. Thanks to the oil, everything fell away easily.

"Fuck, I love you," she said, as we lay there afterwards.

"That's the post coital hormones talking."

"Maybe," she said with a grin, "but it's still true."

"Well, I love you too." I reached out and gave her ass a squeeze. "Particularly certain parts of you."

She punched me playfully. "Now who's talking with their hormones?"

We snuggled together for a while, enjoying the come-down. Gradually, her breathing softened, and I assumed she'd fallen asleep, but then she spoke.

"I can't wait until this is all over."

"Me too," I said, running a hand through her hair. "I know this is rough, but you're dealing with it really well. I'm proud of you. And I'm so damn lucky you're putting up with it at all."

"You *are* rather lucky." She opened her eyes and gazed up at me, a playful little smile playing on her lips. "Then again, so am I." She let out a little sigh. "I'm just not much of a homebody, you know? Before all of this, if I wasn't at work in the evenings, I was out with Ruth and Lou, or Elle, or you. I can't wait to have that again. I want to be able to go out to dinner with you on my arm and watch all the other women in the place drool."

"If that's the case I dare say we'll be rendering the whole place incapacitated. You obviously don't see how most men look at you."

She laughed. "Perhaps in the interests of public safety we'd better stay here, forever, then."

"Perhaps." Some of my mirth slid away. "It won't always be like this, Sophia. We'll fix this, eventually."

"I know," she replied, but there was a hint of sadness in her voice.

I wished I could reassure her, but the truth was, I wasn't sure myself.

Chapter 10

Sebastian

Thomas intercepted me the next morning, as I was arriving at the house.

"Can I have a word?" he asked. He looked concerned.

I motioned him towards my office.

"What's up?" I asked, as he closed the door.

"I heard something last night from one of our guys overseas. It's just a rumour, nothing concrete, but word on the street is that The Syndicate might be planning something big."

My eyes widened. The Syndicate were one of the closest things we had to a rival. They were less tightly knit than us, more of a financial conglomerate than anything else, but that only made them more ruthless. Russia, China, Saudi Arabia - anywhere with big oil or natural gas production - those were their strongholds. We'd had an uneasy peace with them for decades, mostly because butting heads would cause both of us immense damage; but it certainly wasn't beyond the realm of possibility that they were behind the recent attacks.

"Any idea what?" I asked.

Thomas shook his head. "It's just whispers at this point. It may not even be connected to all of this."

"You don't sound like you believe that."

He smiled thinly. "You know me. I don't like coincidences."

"Me either. I can't see an end game in it for them, though," I said. "We're not remotely close to any of their power bases. Even if they did manage to somehow destroy us all down here, it wouldn't make any difference to their operations. If they were going to make a play, I'd expect them to go after Europe or America, not us."

"Maybe they're just sending a message?"

"Maybe," I replied, although that didn't feel quite right. These attacks felt targeted and meticulous. "If it is them, they've certainly upped their game. They're not exactly the most subtle group, but the people messing with us right now are like ghosts. They're always one step ahead."

Thomas nodded. "That's been bothering me too."

"Well, keep your ear to the ground. Maybe they'll slip up and give themselves away. We could use a gift like that, right now. This whole situation is really starting to wear on me. Not to mention the toll it's taking on Sophia."

My discussion with her had been on my mind all day. I desperately wanted her to be happy, and would have liked nothing more than to spend our nights out on the town, but that was a spectacular way to leave us both exposed. Leaving her alone at work was bad enough, but at least her office had door scanners and security guards and a thousand sets of watchful eyes. Bars and restaurants were a different story. They weren't contained, they weren't a known quantity. Even with our little rag tag security team, there were a million things that could go wrong.

But as the afternoon rolled around, I was struck by an idea. I tracked down Tony and Aaron, and organised for them to just go straight back to the house. Tonight, I'd be playing chauffeur.

A few hours later, I was waiting on the footpath outside Sophia's office. As she exited the building and caught sight of me, her face lit up with a curious smile.

"Hey you," she said.

"Hey yourself."

"To what do I owe this pleasure?"

I grinned and held up the bag I was carrying. "I thought maybe we could have a little dinner party in your office. Just because we can't go to a restaurant doesn't mean we can't eat out."

"Oooh, my office. How exotic!" Her voice was sarcastic, but her smile only widened.

"Well, we don't have to..." I replied, trying my best to sound put out.

She laughed. "I'm kidding. That's very sweet of you. And good timing. I'm starving."

I followed Sophia back inside, drawing a few strange looks from her colleagues, but we made it to the office without any awkward questions.

"It's still kind of early," she said, as I closed the door. "What happens if my boss decides to pop round for a chat?"

"Then I will politely ask him to leave."

"He might not appreciate that."

"Well I might not appreciate him interrupting our date."

She laughed. "I suspect you may just win that encounter."

I reached into the bag and cracked open a container. The room instantly filled with the smell of peanuts and garlic. "I hope Thai is okay."

She made an appreciative noise. "Thai is more than

okay."

"And the coup de grace," I said, pulling out the bottle of wine I'd brought.

She clapped. "You know me too well."

"Only plastic cups I'm afraid."

"What?" she replied, with mock haughtiness. "This is an outrage!"

We settled in, passing containers back and forth and shovelling food into our mouths with those thin, store provided chopsticks. We were ravenous, and within just a few minutes we'd both managed to drip sauce down the fronts of our clothes, but all it did was make us laugh. There was something so comfortable about this sort of sharing. I'd eaten at a lot of fancy restaurants in my day, and while they had their charms, none of them compared to this. This was a level of affection and intimacy I assumed I'd never have, but by some miracle of God or fate, or whatever you want to call it, I'd found a woman who seemed to be willing to take all of my baggage on board. And amazingly, with our lives currently wrapped up in conspiracy and danger, we could still share moments like these.

"Thank you for this," she said, as we were taking a breather.

I shrugged. "It's no Mi Casa."

She reached out to give my hand a little squeeze. "Maybe not, but it's perfect anyway." And she was right.

It was a little sad, heading back to our makeshift fortress, but that couldn't erase the joy of the evening. Sophia's eyes were sparkling more than any time since before she was taken, and that alone made me incredibly happy. She had such life in her, and at times I was terrified the situation would crush that to dust.

It was dark by the time we pulled into the driveway, but

I could still see the silhouettes of one of our guards sitting in his car on the grass to one side. The other would be around the back. It was encouraging to see that, even when we weren't home and they had every opportunity to slack off, they didn't. They were true professionals.

I parked the car and we hopped out. Thumbing the door scanner, I opened it and ushered Sophia inside.

"Home sweet home," she said.

I followed her, my eyes shamelessly glued to her ass. She turned her head and caught me. "And what are you looking at?"

"You," I replied. "Or rather, a specific part of you." I gave her a gentle little smack.

"What ever happened to look but don't touch?" she asked coyly.

"I plan on doing a lot more than touching."

I reached up to slip my jacket off, and then everything happened at once. There was a light, scraping sound from somewhere to our left. It was barely more than a whisper, a shoe catching a piece of furniture maybe, but my body had been on twenty four hour alert since this all started, so it was enough to set adrenaline exploding through my veins. If I hadn't already been removing my suit, I wouldn't have got there in time, but my gun was holstered in a shoulder strap that hung just below my armpit. As the two men appeared in the kitchen doorway, their own weapons pointed in our direction, I was already moving. My hand closed around my pistol grip as I lurched to one side, instinctively throwing myself in front of Sophia, knocking her into the room behind us. The air was suddenly thick with hot lead and the scent of gunpowder.

The first man missed his mark entirely, his bullets zinging into the plaster around me, and he paid the price as my first shot took him in the chest. However the next man was better. As his partner collapsed he took careful aim and fired a single round. I felt the wind of it plough past me as I threw myself behind the lounge room wall. Two inches to the left and I'd have been done.

I landed awkwardly and scuttled up into a crouch, then spun to check on Sophia. She looked over at me from the other side of the doorway, her face a mask of terror. I did my best to seem calm and collected, but blood was pounding in my ears. It had been a long time since I'd been in a real combat situation. I'd forgotten how sharp everything gets, how your heart feels like a fist pummelling the inside of your chest.

At any moment Tony and Aaron should have been bursting in through the doors, drawn by the sound of gunfire. But everything remained ominously silent. After a few seconds, I knew we were on our own.

I didn't understand how everything had gone so horribly wrong, but now wasn't the time to think. Now was a time for action. With every passing second, the situation grew more dangerous. Our opponent had gone quiet now. Probably holing up, to wait us out. He had a good position and a tiny space to watch. The moment I peeked out, I'd be done.

If I'd been alone, I could have simply looped around behind him through the lounge room's other doorway, but Sophia was essentially trapped in the corner. She couldn't go anywhere without exposing herself, which meant neither could I. I'd die before I left her alone.

I wracked my brains for some kind of plan, but nothing came. It would have to be a straight shoot out. That was the only way. He'd hit me, but maybe it wouldn't be lethal, maybe I'd still be able to take him out before I collapsed. I might not make it, but Sophia would.

She was still staring at me with those wide, beautiful eyes, her handbag clutched against her chest like a baby. I nodded reassuringly at her, trying to etch every line of that perfect face into my mind, then I crept to the edge of the doorway. She gasped as she realised what I was about to do, but I silenced her with a raised finger against my lips. There was no other option.

Taking a deep breath, I counted to three and then launched myself out across the doorway, the barrel of my pistol panning wildly for a target.

I expected to hear gunfire. I expected to feel that hot metal sting as he calmly picked me off from his perfect vantage. But instead, nothing happened.

The room across the hall was empty.

For a second I was confused, but then panic seized me, and everything suddenly seemed to slip into slow motion as I realised what had happened. I turned my head, catching sight of the man's profile in the lounge room's other doorway as he carefully took aim at me. I'd underestimated him. He hadn't been content to wait it out. Instead he was the one who'd looped around behind.

My gun was still pointed the other way. I tried desperately to bring it around, but my arm felt leaden and impossibly heavy, like I was dragging it through thick mud. His finger twitched toward the trigger. I wasn't going to make it.

And then, when he was surely just milliseconds from firing, a percussion of loud cracks rang out from the corner of the room. Plaster floured the air, and the man's expression went loose. As the red punctures on his chest began to blossom out across his shirt, his legs caved underneath him, and he fell limply to the floor.

For several moments, all I could do was stare. I'd been resigned. In my head, we were already dead, and it took a while for me to understand that that wasn't the case.

I turned slowly to Sophia. The gun I'd given her was still trembling in her hands. Every part of her was shaking in fact. She'd emptied the entire clip, only hitting him twice, but that was all it had taken.

The pistol dropped to the floor. "He was going to shoot you," she said woodenly.

That jolted me back to reality. Glancing over at each body once more to check for movement, I stumbled over and wrapped her in my arms. "I know. I know. You had no choice."

She nodded slowly, although her eyes were still distant. She was the strongest woman I'd ever met, but killing is something you can never be prepared for. It changes you. I couldn't believe I'd put her in that position.

I pulled her against me tightly, stroking her hair. She was in shock, and really needed time to recover, but that wasn't a luxury we had yet. For now I had to comfort her enough so we could move.

The fight felt like it had taken hours, but I knew from experience it was probably only about fifteen seconds. Still, we had to leave. There was a good chance that even through the solid walls someone had heard the shots. The police would likely be on the way, and spending several hours clearing up the mess would only serve to leave us more exposed. Then of course there were our assassins to consider. Things had just gone up to a whole new level, and I doubted that whoever was responsible would suddenly back down just because they'd lost this fight. More men could be on their way. We had to get somewhere safe.

"Sophia, look at me. We need to move now, okay?"

She turned slowly and stared for several seconds, before eventually blinking several times and nodding. "Okay. I'm okay. Let's go."

After scooping up our two weapons, as well as those of our assailants, I led her into the study. "Just getting some supplies," I said, removing my emergency duffel from the bottom of the cupboard.

She didn't reply.

Unzipping the bag I surveyed the contents; two changes of clothes for each of us, cash, phones, passports, and a laptop computer. I'd hoped to God we wouldn't have any cause to run, but I'd been prepared nonetheless.

I withdrew one of the phones and powered it on. It was a cheap, prepaid model, bought from a convenience store. In other words, it was utterly untraceable to me.

I guided Sophia back towards the front door, pausing briefly to snap pictures of the two men. Even as my brain struggled to process what had just happened, the logical part of my mind was still firing on some level. We couldn't stay, so I had to collect whatever evidence I could.

The air outside was warm and heavy. Raising my gun, I scanned the yard slowly, searching for any further danger. It was unlikely — it made more sense for our enemies to just stay together and ensure the job got done — but I wasn't taking any risks.

The garden appeared to be empty.

I started moving towards the gate with Sophia in tow. I could see how hard she was trying. The expression on her face was constantly shifting from frightened confusion to grim determination as she battled to keep her emotions in check.

As we passed the security guys' car, I couldn't help but glance over, already knowing what I'd find. From a distance nothing had looked wrong, but up close, it was Tony's shocked expression that greeted me. He wasn't moving. The red misting on his skin was lit up vividly in the moonlight like a poster for a horror film. Aaron would be around the back somewhere, in a similar state. I felt a hollowness building inside me, but I shoved it to the back of my mind. Not now.

Sophia followed my gaze, and let out a little cry, but I reached out and seized her chin, pulling her eyes to mine. "Don't look." She trembled a little in my grip, her eyes glistening and impossibly wide. "Don't look," I said again. And after a moment, her expression hardened and she gave a curt nod.

"We're going to take a taxi," I said, as we headed up the street. The house was only a five minute walk from the main road. It would be easy to flag down a cab at this time of night. "We need to get somewhere private. For all I know, the car is bugged. I need your phone too."

Her brow furrowed slightly, but she pulled it from her purse and handed it over. I threw it, along with my own personal one, into a bush. "Can't be too careful." I handed her the second prepaid. "Use this instead. I've got one too. The number is already programmed in."

To her credit, she simply nodded again. I was partially awed and partially sickened at how quickly she was becoming used to this.

As I'd suspected, a cab was easy to find. I directed the driver towards Newtown, towards Sophia's house. That wasn't where we were really headed, but I had no idea how many resources our enemies had anymore. I wanted to keep them on their toes.

Once on King Street, we jumped out and hailed another taxi. "North," was all I said to the driver.

Sophia took my paranoia in stride, sitting and staring out the windows, hugging herself lightly despite the warmth. I didn't know what I could say, so I stayed quiet too.

The ocean fanned out in front of us, as we drove out over

the Harbour Bridge, but my mind was racing too fast to appreciate the view. When we arrived at the mini-CBD that is North Sydney, I ushered Sophia out once more and then, picking a random direction, we began to walk. I figured if I did everything as randomly as possible, it made the chances of someone guessing where we'd gone almost impossible.

Two blocks later we found a hotel. It wasn't particularly big, nor were the rooms particularly nice. Sterile was probably the best word to describe it. Cheap furniture, cream coloured linen, and the slightly sickly scent of lemon detergent in the air. People didn't come to this part of town to holiday. They flew in on rushed overnight business trips, their only requirements a clean bed and a well-stocked mini bar. The mere fact that we were a couple checking in together drew a raised eyebrow from the concierge.

The moment I closed the door behind us, something seemed to drain out of Sophia again. She sat down on the bed and turned to face me. "I thought you said that place was safe."

I exhaled slowly. "I thought it was. Nobody should have been able to get in there."

"So what does that mean?"

I could see she already knew the answer. I almost couldn't muster the words, words that had been playing in the back of my mind since the moment the fight ended. "It means you were right," I said slowly. "Someone in the group wants us dead." Despite how obvious it was, hearing myself say it out loud was like a punch to the stomach. One of my brothers had betrayed me. It was inconceivable.

Sophia closed her eyes briefly, like she'd just realised how little she wanted to be right this time. "So what do we do now?"

I shook my head, a sense of hopelessness clawing at my

stomach. "I don't know." And it was true. I had no idea what our next move was. Without knowing who to trust, I couldn't properly use the group's resources. I was effectively cut off. Before, it had been our team against theirs, but now, it was the two of us against the world.

She gave a little nod, like she'd been expecting that, then slipped off her shoes and curled up on the bed. I stood there, staring at this broken woman, feeling so completely ashamed. The signs had been there, but I'd been too blind to see them, and once again she'd nearly paid the price.

"Can you hold me?" she said, after a few seconds. The tremble in her voice was enough to break my heart.

Hurrying towards her I lay down, looping my arm under her neck to cradle her against me. "Hey, hey, it's okay." She didn't cry, she simply burrowed against me, as if she were trying to disappear beneath my skin.

I kissed her forehead softly. "Don't worry, we'll work something out." I filled my voice with as much confidence as possible. What else could I do?

"Okay."

We lay there like that for a few minutes, enjoying the security of each other's presence. Despite my calm facade, the night's events had shaken me. I'd had a little combat exposure back in the day, but nothing ever makes getting shot at any easier. I knew it would pass, but right now, every nerve in my body felt frayed and agitated.

"We should get some rest," I said. "We can deal with this tomorrow. We'll think better with a night's sleep in us."

"Okay," she said again.

I leaned down to kiss her goodnight. It was an instinctive gesture. I hadn't planned for anything to come of it, but the moment our lips touched, a massive current sizzled between us. The lingering adrenaline from our fight surged in my veins, driving my body against hers as though she might be ripped away from me at any second. She was hesitant for a moment, but then she was kissing me back with equal urgency, a fearful hunger that was heartbreaking and yet utterly beautiful. The air swirled, heady with our need; the need to feel each other, to affirm we were both here and safe and together. That somehow, we'd survived.

Our hands fumbled for each other's clothes, tearing them free, and I lowered my naked form over hers, sinking into her wet heat. She arched beneath me, drawing a long intoxicated breath as our bodies joined.

I pulled her against me, welding her form to mine, desperate to be as close to her as humanly possible. There was nothing sensual or controlled about our lovemaking. It was raw and desperate and devastatingly passionate. There were no words to express the way we both felt in that moment, but our bodies could say what our mouths could not. After the terror of what we'd just been through, I desperately wanted to feel something good, something pure, and I wanted her to feel the same.

We came together, our eyes locked, our muscles quivering in unison. We didn't speak when it was over. We just lay there, bathing in the tender glow that, at least temporarily, kept the darkness at bay.

Chapter 11

Sophia

For a few minutes after I woke, I actually felt really good. It was one of those lazy awakenings, where things come to you gradually; the sun through the window, the warmth of the blanket, the weight and scent of Sebastian besides me. Soon enough though, everything else made itself known.

Thinking back over it all, I felt strangely numb about the whole thing. I didn't know if that was normal or not. I'd killed a man. It seemed like I should have been balled up in a corner somewhere. But I wasn't. Maybe if I'd still been living my ordinary life, blissfully ignorant of this world, it would have been different. But given everything that was going on around us, it somehow didn't seem so shocking. He'd been trying to kill us, and I'd stopped him. That was all there was to it. I suspected it would come to haunt me, in time, but at that moment, I felt eerily calm. Perhaps it was just my body doing what it needed to, to get through this thing.

I glanced over at Sebastian's sleeping form, my eyes drinking in the taut coils of his back. It made me feel a little perverted that even now, the first thing I did was check him out, but the memory of our recent love making was blaring like fireworks behind my eyes. I had to admit, being shot at did have its perks. Our coupling had never been like that before; so raw, so desperate. He'd loved me like he might never get another chance, and my body had responded in kind.

He woke a few minutes later and rolled towards me, smiling through sleepy eyes. "Hey."

"Hey," I replied.

He leaned in to kiss me, and for a second I thought we might be taken by the same manic combustion that had seized us last night, but I had to settle for a little tingle in my belly instead. The crushing fear that had fuelled us appeared to be all burnt up.

"I'm starving," he said.

"Me too."

He slipped out from under the sheet and walked to the mini-bar. "Well, we can either have Snickers for breakfast, or we can venture out."

"You think that's safe?" I asked.

He shrugged and nodded. "It's going to be buzzing out there pretty soon. Finding two people in suits will be needle in haystack territory. Besides, nobody has any idea where we are. We're off the grid."

I glanced out the window. He was right. The streets were already thronging with people. North Sydney is the biggest business district outside of the actual CBD, making it a perfect disguise for people dressed like we were.

We found a little cafe in a side street and snagged a table in the back corner. We'd missed the breakfast rush and the place was starting to empty out, so if we talked quietly enough, we had a little privacy.

"So, what's our plan?" I said, when our waitress was out of earshot. She'd brought coffee, and I could already feel the sweet rush of caffeine wending its way through my brain. I was alert and ready as I was ever going to be to work out our next move.

He blinked several times, apparently taken aback by my directness. It was then that I noticed how tired he looked. The little lines that webbed their way out from his eyes were more pronounced than normal and his expression was slightly slack. I suspected he hadn't got much rest last night.

"I'm not entirely sure," he said.

"Well, let's work out what we know. We know that someone from Alpha sent those men to our house, correct?"

He closed his eyes briefly and nodded. "Nobody else could have gotten in there, let alone known where it was."

"Okay, so that gives us something to aim at."

"Kind of, yeah," he replied. "But whoever it is, they're smart. When they kidnapped you, we threw everything we could at them, and we came up blank. Property ownership, the identity of the thugs they'd hired, everything. It was like trying to track down a ghost. Assuming that they're still that competent, I doubt we're going to find them easily."

I knew this conversation was difficult for him, but there was no way to avoid it. "Well, surely some members are bigger candidates than others?"

He understood instantly. "You mean Ewan?"

I nodded. "It was pretty clear from the outset that he didn't exactly approve of me. What did you say he called me? A liability? If those aren't the words of a man who wants me out of the picture, I don't know what are."

His brow furrowed, and he let out a long breath. "I know he seems like the obvious candidate, but I just can't see it. Maybe he'd move against *us*, maybe, but even that's a stretch.

And Charlie and Simon? I'd bet a million to one he'd never do that. They were his closest friends. They'd been in the group together for decades."

"People can surprise us in the worst ways, sometimes," I said.

I could see him trying to make the pieces fit in his head, but eventually he shook his head. "You didn't see his face, hear his anger when he heard about their deaths. Besides, why would he be upset with you for endangering the group if he was also working to destroy it?"

He had a point. That didn't quite stack up. "So what about the others?"

He stared desolately down at the table. "I don't know. I can't really believe it of any of them. The group is a brother-hood, Sophia. I've known them all for years. I can't see any of them just turning power hungry all of a sudden."

"So that's what you think it's all about? Power?"

"Maybe. None of it really adds up. Taking out a few council members, sure, I guess I can see that as part of a larger plan, but then why go after you? That part still puzzles me."

I nodded. "Me too."

The waitress arrived with our food, and we ate in thoughtful silence for a few minutes.

"Let's try a different approach," I said eventually. "Who knew you were coming to my office last night?"

His eyes widened a fraction as he realised my implication. "Of course. I missed that. Whoever it was must have known we'd be out late. Every other night we arrived separately, and at different times. It would have been a nightmare to coordinate."

"Exactly. They saw an opportunity, and they jumped on it."

His expression slipped. "The only person I told was

Thomas," he said, a current of disbelief running through his voice. "I'm not exactly on friendly chatting terms with many people over there right now. But there's no way he'd... he's my closest friend." He closed his eyes momentarily, collecting his thoughts. "There were other people in the room at the time. We'd just finished a meeting. I didn't really pay attention to who might be listening in, but plenty of them could have overheard."

"So it could be any of them," I said.

He nodded. "That does limit it to the inner council only though. There was no one else in the room."

"Well, that's something." I weighed our options. "So, we obviously can't go back to the house and, I take it from the way you threw away our phones, using the Alpha network at all is also off the cards?"

"I'm afraid so. They'd find us in an instant."

"So do we have any options at all? Or are we destined to discard our identities and live out of hotels forever?"

"It's not quite that bleak," he replied. "There's a few things we can try. I've got pictures of the men from last night, as well as their weapons. I can send that info off to some of my contacts directly, without going through Alpha at all. Like I said before, I doubt the bad guys are sloppy enough to leave a trail, but it's worth a shot."

I nodded. "Okay."

"Also, Joe should be on his way back right now, and he might be able to help us."

I raised an eyebrow. "I thought we weren't trusting the group right now."

"Joe is a special case. I've known him for my entire adult life. He recruited me, for God's sake. I'm one hundred percent certain he's got nothing to do with this."

The firmness of his tone left no room for argument and,

the truth was, I trusted Joe too. "Fair enough," I said.

"We might be able to use his Alpha connection to see if whoever broke into our house left any evidence. Theoretically there should be security footage and a thumbprint record. I expect it's been cleaned up, but you never know."

"Okay," I said again. It seemed like a solid plan, given the circumstances. Then I had another idea. "Have you considered just announcing to the group that someone has gone rogue? Maybe you'll spook the spy and make him do something stupid."

"I thought about it. It might work, but it also might also have the opposite effect. If everyone suspects everyone, all sense of order will break down, and the chaos might help our enemy instead of hurt them. That's not a risk I'm willing to take unless we have no choice. The group is in enough danger already."

That made sense. "Alright."

We finished our food in contemplative silence.

"You know, a tiny part of me is regretting not taking those plane tickets right now," I said.

He managed a tiny smile. "I'm not surprised. The offer's still open, you know. I got you a passport made up just in case."

"Ooh, do I have a code name?"

"From memory, you're Lucy Page."

I made a face. "Makes me sound like a TV housewife from the fifties."

He chuckled. "Sorry."

"In any case, I'm certainly not going to go lie on any tropical beaches while you're stuck here, battling evil. You could come with me, though. Star crossed lovers fleeing to a foreign land together. It's kind of romantic."

He smiled wistfully. "I wish I could."

I'd said it like I was joking, but I'd be lying if I said the thought hadn't crossed my mind. Maybe running off together was the best solution. Would it really be so bad, starting over from scratch? "Have you ever thought about leaving?"

He didn't reply straight away. "I hadn't, but then I met you."

Such a short sentence, but it resonated through me.

"But it's daunting, you know?" he continued. "The group has been my life for so long. I don't know what I'd do without it."

I nodded. I understood that particular fear all too well.

"Anyway," he said, signalling for the cheque, "we should get back to the hotel. It will take a while for my contacts to get back to me, so the sooner we start, the sooner we might get some results."

A few minutes later we were back in the room. While he was sending off the info to his contacts, I fired through an email to my boss using my new phone, explaining that I'd come down violently ill and needed a few days off. He replied almost instantly saying it was no trouble. I got the sense he was extremely pleased to have me back at all, so a few more days made little difference. I didn't know what I'd do if our exile stretched into weeks, or longer, but I figured I'd cross that bridge when I came to it.

Once we'd both taken care of business, it was just a matter of waiting. I'd thought being penned up in the Alpha house was frustrating, but something about the cheap, cut and paste hotel decor made that room feel incredibly oppressive. We lay on the bed drinking wine from the mini-bar and watching daytime TV. I'd bought a few magazines on the way back, and I tried leafing through them, but I couldn't make myself focus. I was restless and frustrated at how powerless we were.

At some point, Sebastian fell asleep. Apparently he really

had been wiped out. I tried to join him, but my body would-n't cooperate. Instead, I found myself turning the situation over and over in my mind. I wished I'd paid better attention to Sebastian's colleagues. There were only a few who I'd even really talked with and, of that group, nothing stood out - be-sides Ewan's blatant dislike. Trey seemed friendly and rela-tively harmless and besides, he wasn't a council member. Then there was Thomas who, while being a little intense at times, appeared to care about Sebastian. Some of the other men had certainly seemed a little cold towards us, but I put that down more to Ewan's influence than anything else. Who-ever the mole was, they were doing an amazing job of blend-ing in.

At about six thirty, Sebastian woke up. "Sorry, I didn't mean to sleep."

"It's fine, you looked like you needed it."

He nodded and flashed me a half smile. "I'll make it up to you by getting dinner. There's a Chinese place just down-stairs that does takeaway."

I glanced at the TV, feeling a tightness in my chest. The prospect of spending any more time here, stewing in the hor-ror that had become our lives, was almost too much to bear. I already felt like I was losing my mind and, if I stayed here, all I'd be able to think about was how helpless we were. "What we should do is hit the town," I said.

I'd mostly been joking, but the moment the words left my lips, the idea took root in my head. The gradually bloom-ing smile on Sebastian's face said he felt the same way. "Maybe we should."

I laughed. "Is that crazy?" It seemed ridiculous to consider going out on a date, given everything that was happening, but hell, if people were going to be constantly trying to kill me, I felt like maybe I should take advantage of the lulls in between.

Besides, I could desperately use the distraction.

"A little, maybe, but I can't see it being a problem as long as we keep it low key. If anybody had managed to follow us, they'd have made their move by now. A hotel is hardly going to provide much of an obstacle for one of my brothers. So we can assume they have no idea where we are. As far as they know, we could be anywhere in the city. Maybe anywhere in the country."

It made sense. "Low key hey?" I said. "Like pizza and a movie?"

"That sounds perfect."

A few minutes later, we were walking out through the hotel's front door. The streets were emptier at night, but there was still a steady stream of office workers who were clocking off late or heading home after a few end of day drinks.

It took us a while to find a pizza place, but when we did, we struck gold. A few blocks away from the main thoroughfare, we stumbled upon a tiny shop front with a giant neon pizza slice flickering above it. There was no other signage, not even a name, but it seemed to have what was important. It wasn't until we made our way inside that we realised what a gem we'd discovered.

The scene before us looked like it had been ripped straight out of a nineties sitcom. Dimly lit booths with red and white plastic table cloths, walls plastered with yellowed band posters and old advertisements for beer and motor oil. There was even an ancient pinball machine in the corner, it's warbling, high-pitched cries for attention fighting vainly against the throbbing rock music being piped through the speakers.

The place was relatively full, but the smiling, old, Italian-looking waiter didn't seem fazed, guiding us through the tables to an open booth, tucked to one side. Sebastian and I grinned at one another as we sat down. I could already feel some of my tension ebbing away, and I could tell he felt the same way.

We ordered a few pizzas to share, as well as a couple of the foaming mugs of unnamed beer that seemed to be the drink of choice.

"We might have another Mi Casa on our hands," Sebastian said to me once the waiter disappeared.

"We just might," I agreed. "It's almost enough to make you forget..." I trailed off, realising I was only going to kill the mood, but it was too late. His expression wilted.

"I didn't really ask before, but are you coping okay?" he said. "Yesterday... well, it was pretty rough."

Memories of the previous night appeared, unbidden, in my mind. The weight of the gun, the violent kick of it in my hands, the way the man's eyes grew wide as his legs collapsed under him. *Not now!* I pushed it all to the side. "That's one way to put it," I said, keeping my voice level. "But yeah, I think I'm doing okay."

He didn't look like he believed me, but he nodded. "I know the apologies are probably getting old, but I can't tell you how sorry I am that I put you in that position. I should have listened to you when you questioned my colleagues."

"You should have," I said, managing a small smile, "but, like I said, I stopped blaming you for all of this weeks ago. You can't shoulder the burden of everything that happens to the people you know, Sebastian. Proximity doesn't equal fault. I've forgiven you, but our relationship will never work unless you forgive yourself too."

Some of the tension drained out of his face. "You're right. The thought of you being in danger just tears me up, that's all. If I lost you..." he shook his head.

I reached out and weaved my fingers through his. "You

won't. The odds may be bad, but so far, we've survived everything they've thrown at us. We'll get through this, we just need to focus." I wasn't quite as confident as all that, but I knew that he needed to hear it. If, by some miracle, we were to beat this thing, we needed to keep our eyes on the prize.

It seemed to work. After a few seconds, his jaw tightened and he nodded. "That sounds like a plan."

"But not tonight," I continued. "We can't do anything until we hear back from everyone, so tonight, let's forget all about this and just be a couple, out on a date. I want to remember what it's like to feel normal again, even if it's just for one night."

His lips gradually curled upwards. "I can do that."

And so we did. For the next two hours, we talked about everything but the lurking danger. He seemed to enjoy hearing about my antics with the girls and, thankfully, Ruth provided enough material to base an entire sitcom on. Pretty soon we were both in hysterics, our stomachs aching from laughter.

The pizza was spectacular. Thinly cut and dripping with cheese, it tasted as delicious as it did unhealthy, and it was exactly the kind of comfort food I needed.

When we'd had our fill, we caught a cab a few minutes north to the nearest cinema. Out on the street, I found myself glancing over my shoulder a few times, but nobody was paying any attention to us. It appeared Sebastian had been right. We were off the grid.

None of the films playing really looked interesting, but I didn't care. It was more the act of going to the movies than the movie itself. Something about going on such a mundane date with Sebastian pleased me immensely. It felt like the kind of date I'd have gone on with a university boyfriend. There was no fanciness to it, no expectations or desire to impress. It was just the two of us hanging out and enjoying one another's company.

We settled on some big budget sci-fi title that seemed like it might at least look impressive on the big screen. It was a relatively quiet session, with only fifteen or so other people in the cinema. We took up residence somewhere towards the back.

Within about ten minutes, I was bored. It did look spectacular, but the script sounded like it had been written by an internet chatroom bot, and every member of the cast seemed to be too busy practising Blue Steel to actually display any other facial expressions.

Apparently, Sebastian felt the same way. "Is this what counts for cinema these days?" he whispered. "It's been a while since I've been to the movies, so I'm a little out of touch."

I shook my head. "I don't go much either, but this is definitely scraping the bottom of the barrel. I'm not sure I can take another hour and a half."

His eyes took on a wicked glint. "Perhaps I can find a way to make that time a little more bearable." Lifting the armrest so there was nothing between us, he slipped closer, burying his face against my head and breathing in deeply. "I wouldn't want you to be bored," he said, in a soft throaty voice, and before I knew it, his hand was skimming gently up my leg.

I laughed at his audacity and then glanced around. There was another couple in our row, about eight seats over, and a group of three guys just a few rows in front. Nobody was paying any attention to us so far, but it wouldn't take much to change that.

"Sebastian," I said, nodding at the couple and raising my eyebrows.

He grinned like a child who knew he was about to do something naughty and just didn't care. "They're not paying attention." Pulling away momentarily, he shrugged off his jacket and threw it over both our laps. "And if they are, now all they'll see is a cold girl and her chivalrous boyfriend."

Before I could argue, his hand was climbing my thigh once more. I felt like I should keep up the pretence of resistance, but the truth was, my heart was already beating wildly, and the closer he drew to my sex, the less fighting it seemed to matter.

His fingers inched upward until they found my panties, tugging them to the side. The first touch was soft, a gentle caress from my entrance all the way up, and I felt myself grow wet almost instantly. I let out a little sigh and sunk deeper into my seat to give him better access. Taking my cue, he slipped one long finger inside me, teasing and probing until he eventually settled on my g-spot. That sudden contact sent a spike of pleasure through me, drawing a sharp gasp from my lips.

"Uh uh, quiet now," he whispered. "We wouldn't want to alert our audience."

I swallowed loudly and clamped my mouth closed, glancing around the room once more. All eyes were still fixed on the screen, although the couple in our row both looked to be wearing tighter expressions than before. Was it just the film? Or were they onto our game and simply trying to ignore us? I felt an uneasy excitement settle in my stomach, the same kind of perverse thrill I'd experienced wearing the butt plug around my office.

Sebastian stroked me with a slow, rhythmic motion, and everything began turning to liquid inside me. A second finger joined the first, and I bit back another cry, curling my hands tightly around the arm rests for fear that my movements would betray us.

"Do you like that?" Sebastian breathed into my ear. "Do you like being pleasured in a room full of people?"

I nodded quickly, not trusting myself to do more than that.

"God, you feel so good around my fingers. I wish I had something else inside you. But I can wait. I'll fuck you soon enough."

For a moment, all I could think about was having his cock inside me, but then his thumb found my clit, and all other thoughts fled. There was just his hand and the exquisite things it was doing to me. The simultaneous stimulation was incredible. I had no idea how he was so dexterous, but every motion seemed to work together in perfect harmony. A tightness began to build in my core, beckoning, begging for release.

"I want you to come for now me, Sophia, and I want you to do it without making a sound."

I wasn't sure that was going to be possible. Even with my mouth firmly shut, there were shrill little noises escaping my throat. But I sure as hell wasn't going to stop and tell him that.

With the same relentless pace, he brought me over the cusp. I buried my face against his shoulder, my whole body shaking, as though all of the cries I wasn't letting out were bouncing around inside me.

"Fuck," I said when it was over.

He glanced around. "As tempting as that sounds, I think *that* might get us noticed."

I laughed, but the suggestion made my sex clench all the same. "Perhaps we should go somewhere where we won't be noticed then," I said, running my hand slowly along the bulge in his pants

He stiffened and let out a long breath. "And miss this fine excuse for a motion picture?"

I raised my eyebrows. "Well, hey, if you don't want to..."

The intensity returned to those emerald eyes. "You know

what I want?" he said, his voice a dry rasp. "I want you to watch the rest of the film and think about how hard I'm going to fuck you when it's over. I want you squirming in your seat, so wet for me I can smell it."

I swallowed loudly. Yeah, like there was any chance I could think about anything else now. "Okay," I said softly.

We did watch the rest of the film, but I'll be damned if I could tell you a single thing about it.

* * * * *

Sebastian's insistence on waiting had the desired effect. By the time we left the cinema, I was a flustered mess. Judging by the urgency in his walk, I wasn't the only one.

The moment we stepped through the door to our hotel room, I felt his body press up behind mine. My neck lolled to one side automatically, exposing the curve of my neck that I knew he was longing to kiss. He didn't disappoint, ducking his head to brush his lips softly across my skin. I let out a gentle sigh. It was an intimate position; sensual and tender. I used to think sexual familiarity was a sign that things were getting stale, but I loved those little moments with Sebastian, the understanding our bodies shared. If anything, that connection excited me more.

With reverent delicacy his mouth traced a path down one shoulder, and then the other, his fingers stroking my hips, before slinking upwards to toy with my dress straps.

"I want to look at you," he said.

"By all means," I replied.

With two gentle flicks of his wrist, my dress was tumbling to the floor. My bra followed moments later. There was a sharp intake of breath behind me, and then his arms were around me once more.

"Christ I love this position," he said, echoing my earlier thoughts. His hands moved up to cup my breasts, kneading gently, rolling my nipples between his fingers. The yearning in my veins surged, rushing to pool between my legs. "I love having your ass pressed against me while I play with you, knowing I just have to unzip myself and I'd be inside you."

I twisted my hips in response, grinding myself against him, causing his breath to falter. He was certainly ready. I could feel the strength of his excitement, hot and needy, pressing urgently through his pants. "Well I love feeling what I'm doing to you back there," I replied.

"Hmm, is that so?" he said in amusement. "Well, I would be remiss if I didn't check what I'm doing to you."

One of his hands stayed to roam my chest, but the other began to inch slowly, tantalisingly, down my stomach. He slipped inside my panties, parting my folds, my clit swelling with electricity at his touch.

"I do seem to be having the desired effect," he teased.

"That you are," I replied, squirming against him. Although there were no bonds involved, with our bodies arranged that way I was strangely helpless. I couldn't explore him as he explored me. My hands had nowhere to go but to curl around his powerful forearms while he pleasured me. He moved slowly, more a tease than anything else, but I still found my legs growing shaky beneath me.

He withdrew and spun me to face him, silencing my protest with a kiss. Now free to touch him, my hands began to roam, revelling in the coiled power of his body. I wanted to take my time, but I couldn't help but be drawn to the trembling bulge between his legs. I stroked him through the material, generating a deep vibration in the centre of his chest.

"Let's not get ahead of ourselves. There's something else I want you to do before I fuck you."

"Oh?"

"I want you to take a shower."

I gazed at him in bewilderment. "Do I really smell that bad?"

He favoured me with a small smile, but something in the air had shifted. This wasn't a request, it was a command. My skin prickled with anticipation.

"Not at all, I'd just prefer you were clean." There was a heaviness to his tone now, an edge I knew all too well.

"Okay," I said, the sudden rush of endorphins stealing the strength from my voice. I still found it amazing how he could do that with just a slight change in intonation, like a snake charmer mesmerising his cast.

Giving him one final squeeze, I slipped from his arms and sauntered to the bathroom, glancing back over my shoulder, enjoying watching him watch me. The lust in his eyes when he looked at my body never ceased to thrill me.

Once inside, I shut the door and removed my panties. I set the water running and adjusted the temperature before stepping inside. I knew he'd be joining me soon.

However, what happened next managed to surprise me. I heard the click of the door handle, but before I could even turn, the room was plunged into darkness. For a split second I felt a bolt of fear, but then Sebastian spoke. "On second thoughts, we're both rather filthy if you ask me. I believe we could both use a shower."

I laughed. "In the dark?"

"I don't need to see you to make you come, Sophia."

A shiver rolled down my spine. I wasn't sure I'd ever get sick of that dirty mouth. "We'll see about that," I replied, trying to sound coy. "Come on in, then. I'll wash you if you wash me."

"Deal."

In a moment, the glass door was opening and then his hard form was pressing against mine once more, only now he was naked too. The moment we touched, my confusion about the lack of light melted away. Feeling but not seeing him lent the experience a whole new kind of tactility. With my sight stolen, even the slightest contact seemed magnified a hundred times. It was like the blindfold all over again, only this time, both of us were blind.

His kiss was fiercer this time, hungrier, his hands seizing my shoulders while his tongue plundered my mouth. The pressure of his assault drove me backwards until I was pressed up against the wall, the coldness of the tiles contrasting wonderfully with the warmth of the water. He seemed at ease in the dark, but my heart was racing. Every movement, every brush of his hand, was an unexpected surprise. My body was thrumming, every nerve tingling.

Some indeterminable time later, he broke away. "I believe I promised to clean you."

"Oh, you did. You know how much of a dirty girl I am," I said in my best porno voice.

He chuckled. "That I do. Now hold still." I heard the squeeze of a lotion bottle and then something soft yet coarse began stroking my collarbone. Apparently the room came with a wash cloth.

He took his time, working his way gradually down one arm and then the other, scrubbing me with tiny circular motions. The cloth felt wonderful against my skin, a gentle scrape tempered by soap and water. I loved the sense of just being lavished upon. Sebastian may have called the shots in the bedroom, but he certainly never left me feeling neglected.

Soon, he turned his attention to my chest. "This area needs a more personal touch."

I made a little noise of encouragement, my body already

yearning for him to accelerate proceedings.

Squeezing more soap onto his hands he began to massage my breasts. The sensation of them sliding between his fingers, his slickened skin against mine, was exquisite. Judging by the low rumble emanating from the darkness, he was enjoying it too.

He picked up the sponge again to work my stomach, back, and legs, lathering me with a thick layer of suds that he made no effort to wash off. I soon learned why when the stream of water suddenly vanished from above, only to reappear moments later in front of me. I hadn't realised that shower head was detachable.

"I've heard it said that a shower head is a girl's best friend," Sebastian murmured.

"I've never had the chance to try one," I replied, although I was already beginning to believe it might be true. You'd think after a life time of showers, you'd pretty much understand what they're capable of. They're pleasant, soothing, warming, but that's about the extent of it. Only in Sebastian's hands, this became something else entirely. The way he danced the jet across my skin, constantly alternating the pressure, distance, and angle, was incredible. I don't know if it was just the sensuality of the experience, or the darkness, or Sebastian's expert technique, but it left my entire body tingling.

"Then allow me." With obvious relish, he began working his way slowly down my torso, meticulously washing every part. The closer he drew to my aching sex, the more I began to squirm.

"Widen your stance," he ordered, and then suddenly, the stream was between my legs.

"Oh Jesus," I cried. The warmth of it, the relentless rhythm, was like nothing I'd ever experienced before. It was like a thousand tiny fingers, all stroking me at once, and they weren't easing me towards orgasm, they were hurling me through the door as fast as humanely possible.

While the water strummed my clit, he leaned in close, bracing my ass with one hand and drawing my nipple into his mouth, swirling and sucking and nipping softly. I felt my knees begin to buckle, but he held me firmly, bringing the nozzle closer still. The stimulation was almost too much — it rode that impossibly thin line between pleasure and discomfort — but I was beyond caring. Already, everything was beginning to tighten inside me. It was like I could feel each and every drop of water vibrate all the way into my core.

"I'm coming, Sebastian. I'm coming."

He let out an affirmative grunt and sealed his mouth over mine as my climax took hold. Everything seemed to shrink away, then explode outward in a giant, rolling wave of ecstasy. I was glad he was supporting me, because I'm quite sure I would have ended up splayed on the tiles, if he hadn't been.

"So, there may be some merit to that rumour," he said, my body sagging against his.

"I believe so," I replied. "Especially if you're pressed for time. What was that, one minute?"

He laughed. "Something like that."

I felt utterly drained, but being pressed up against him again reminded me that only half our bargain had been fulfilled. "I think it may be my turn with that," I said, fumbling along his arm until I found the shower head. "I'm not the only one that needs a thorough wash."

"If you insist."

Partly out of a desire for revenge, but mostly because I wanted to savour his body, I took my time, painstakingly soaping and rinsing every inch of him. I was getting used to my blindness now, used to the amplified sense of touch it lent me. In the past, with the blindfold, I'd always been in a position of submission, but here I was free to explore. I loved the way his body felt in the water, hard and soft and slick all at once. With only my hands to guide me I roamed across his skin, running them gently over the firm rises of his triceps, the thick slabs of his chest, revelling in every perfect ridge.

Even in the dark, I was constantly aware of his cock. Every so often as I shifted position it would graze against me, sending a bolt of lust shooting through my veins. I enjoyed those little moments of contact, the sharp breaths and soft noises they drew from him.

Soon, I abandoned soap and water all together, slipping in close until my face was against his chest. "I have a special cleaning implement I think would be very effective on you," I purred.

"Is that so?" he said, more than a little strain evident in his voice. I could tell he was close to breaking point.

"It is. Allow me to show you."

Wrapping my hands around the hard globes of his ass, I drew his nipple into my mouth. He gasped and rocked against me, pushing his shaft firmly against my stomach. I teased him like that for half a minute, but soon, I was unable to contain myself any longer. Kissing a trail down his stomach I dropped to my knees and seized his length in my hand. He felt impossibly thick, and seemed to be growing more with every passing moment. I loved how, even with no visual stimulation, he was utterly ready for me; a perfect picture of virility.

He let out a long groan as I took him into my mouth, pumping him from the base and sliding my lips up and down with painstaking slowness. He felt fleshy and soft and I took my time tasting every inch of him, dragging my tongue along the trembling ridge underneath. Heat rushed through his shaft as he swelled further still, but I took it in stride, gradually easing him deeper down my throat.

"Your lips are fucking magic," he said.

I loved being in that position. It was submissive, yet utterly empowering. For the first time since we'd started, I wished the lights were on. I wanted to look at him, to see the pleasure I was giving, to watch his face contort as I gradually brought him undone.

His fingers found my head, tightening around my hair, guiding me and quickening my pace, and for a while I gave control over to him.

Eventually, an idea came to me. "I wonder if this is just for women," I mused, pulling back momentarily, and before he could reply, I aimed the jet of water at his balls and resumed sucking him. The effect was instantaneous. He sunk back against the wall, a long, throaty sound falling from his mouth. Continuing to stroke him with one hand, I began experimenting with the shower head, teasing every part of him as he had me.

"Fuck, Sophia, that's incredible. Don't stop."

Sensing that he was close, I focused my efforts, locking my lips just below his crown and stroking rapidly, keeping the shower head focused strong and close. His body stiffened and he let out a single guttural roar, then spurted down my throat. His orgasm seemed to last forever, and I pumped furiously, milking every drop.

"Jesus Christ," he said, his voice ragged. "That was a huge load."

I giggled and nodded, still tasting him on my tongue.

"I may have to have one of these installed," he said.

"You won't hear me object."

He reached out to take my arms, pulling me to my feet. "Put it back for now. I want to fuck you under the water."

I was only too happy to oblige. My exploration of his

body had left me aching for him.

Once the nozzle was back in place, he spun me around and positioned himself behind me. "Brace yourself against the wall," he said. "I'm done being gentle." The way he said that made my sex clench.

I did as commanded, laying my hands on the tiles, and in a moment he was pushing inside me. I let out a long breath. There was no initial sting now, no moment of accommodation. He fit inside me as though he'd always been there, as though he'd never left. There was a sense of completeness to that moment that I'd never felt with anyone else. A transcendence, where physical pleasure rose up and became something more.

From the moment he entered me, I could tell he was going to be true to his word. Each thrust of his hips was long and hard, and my body shook with the impact. After such exquisite foreplay, it was exactly what I wanted. An explosion of all of our pent up desire.

With my body angled upward, each punishing thrust stroked the bundle of nerves at my core, sending ripples of pleasure rolling through me. The air around us was heavy with steam, and I drew it into my lungs, savouring the warmth as it flowed through me.

Wrapping one hand around my hip, he seized my hair with the other, tugging my head backwards and sending a delicious sting through my scalp. There was something so raw about being fucked like that, standing up, darkness all around, my body trapped roughly in his grip. The ferocity of his movements hurt a little, but that only excited me more.

The sounds emanating from his throat were low, almost bestial, as he took from me what I'd been teasing all night. His size meant I could feel every pulse of lust, every firm ridge and soft edge.

"I promised I was going to fuck you hard," he said, pausing momentarily only to hammer back into me again.

"You did," I replied, although they barely sounded like words.

"Is this what you wanted?"

"You know it is."

The heat inside me continued to build. It was a raging fire. Impossible to ignore. My muscles began to contract, but there was nowhere for them to go. His hardness was everywhere, filling me, stretching me, claiming me. As my moans sunk lower in my throat there was a flooding sensation in my brain and that fire suddenly exploded. It shot out from my toes to my head, leaving me trembling and gasping for air.

A few moments later, he came too. There was a rush of heat, then a roar, and then his fingers were biting into my side as he slammed himself into me, forcing my whole body against the wall.

"Christ," he said, when his hips finally slowed.

"Mmmm."

He pulled out of me, and despite the slight sting of my now raw flesh, my body complained at the absence. Spinning me around, he trapped my lips in a kiss.

"And that is why we wait."

I laughed. "That's easy to say now."

His hands found my ass, and he gave a little squeeze. "I wouldn't worry too much. If I'm being totally honest I can never resist you for very long. And when this is all over, I plan on spending more time inside you than out."

"Well now, that's exactly what a girl wants to hear."

Chapter 12

Sophia

When I woke the next morning, Sebastian was already up. He was sitting in the room's only chair already fully dressed, idly thumbing his chin and staring off into space.

"Morning," I said.

He jolted a little. "Oh. Good morning."

"Everything okay?" I asked, stretching lazily.

"Yeah, everything's fine. Better than fine, really."

I slid down the bed and sat in front of him. "Oh yeah, how's that?"

He held up the prepaid phone that had been hidden in his other hand. "We've got something. My guy at the Federal Police ran our attackers' faces through their database and actually came back with matches."

The look on his face told me that perhaps this wasn't all good news. "Well that's great, right? Who were they?"

He gave a non-committal nod. "Our would-be killer seems to be working on his own, because he didn't use Alpha guys. It looks like he farmed the job out and basically hired two hit men. Those two guys were known muscle for Anton Silva, who is suspected to be one of the biggest crime bosses in the country."

"Wow. Okay. Just another small fish then."

He shot me a smile, but it was short lived.

"So what do we do with that info?" I asked.

His lips compressed and he let out a little sigh. "I'm still working that out. This guy is the real deal, Sophia. Drugs, weapons, prostitution; he runs it all. If we play it right, we may be able to use him to get to whoever wants us dead, but one misstep..."

He didn't need to finish the sentence. I could fill in the blanks. I felt a lump building in my throat, but I nodded anyway. "I get it. Bad guy."

"Bad guy," Sebastian confirmed. "Anyway, Joe is on his way, so we can talk about it more when he arrives, but I think our best bet is to just try and buy Silva off. He's a criminal, which means he has a price. Everyone has a price."

"But how do we get him to take the money without killing us in the process? I mean, he was hired to take us out and he screwed it up. We can't exactly just show up at his doorstep."

Sebastian stared me dead in the eye. "Actually, that's exactly what I'm thinking I might do."

I searched his voice for humour, but found none. "Are you insane?"

This time he smiled. "A little, maybe. But I think it will work. He's not going to just gun me down on sight, not if I give him the right incentive first. He may be ruthless, but you don't get where he is unless you're practical as well. He'll hear me out, probably figuring he can finish the job afterwards if he doesn't like what he hears."

"That's a lot of assumptions for us to risk our lives on."

He gave a heavy nod. "I know. But what other choice do we have? Joe's searches came back empty. Our enemy holds all the cards, and this is the only lead we've got. If we want our lives back, I don't see any other option."

I wracked my brains for an alternative. "I don't suppose we could just call Silva? Avoid putting ourselves in the firing line?"

Sebastian barked out a laugh. "I can call to set up the meet, but getting Silva himself on the phone will be all but impossible. You don't become a criminal kingpin by discussing organised murder over the phone."

My cheeks reddened. That made sense.

As much as it scared me to admit, I realised he was right. We'd been on the back foot for so long and we'd stay there, unless we took a chance. This might be our last opportunity. But, beyond that, I was sick of running, sick of being hunted. If I was going to be put in danger again, I wanted it to be on my terms.

"Okay, if you think we can pull it off, then I'm sold," I said. "But don't think for one second that just because you kept saying 'I' while I was saying 'we' that you're going in there alone."

His expression hardened. "There's no need for both of us to take the risk. I'm not going to let you put yourself in danger because of my mistakes anymore."

"Well I'm not letting you walk into that death trap by yourself," I countered. "You think it's any easier for *me* seeing *you* put yourself at risk? If you went in there and didn't come out, it would rip me open knowing that I might have be able to do something. I may not have much experience with this sort of thing, but last time shit hit the fan, I stepped up. Maybe I can be useful again." It amazed me how easily I was able to talk about that incident. Maybe I really was becoming desensitised.

I put a hand on his knee. "We're in this together, Sebastian. Whatever happens."

He stared at me for a full ten seconds, somehow managing to look touched yet incredibly anxious. Eventually, though, he broke into a sad little smile. "Together it is, then," he said softly, reaching out to squeeze my hand. And somehow it felt like an incredibly tender moment, instead of an insane suicide pact. Yep, definitely desensitised.

Joe arrived a short time later and we went out for breakfast to discuss everything. He sat, wearing an unreadable expression, while Sebastian recounted everything that had happened so far. He'd heard the short version, but now he was getting the gory details.

"If you have any other suggestions, I'm all ears," said Sebastian, when the story was over.

Joe pondered. He didn't even look surprised. "Nothing springs to mind," he said eventually. "Whoever this is, they're not making many mistakes. When I looked through our system, I couldn't find any loose ends. According to the database, nobody besides you and your team swiped into your Alpha house. They cleared everything. If we don't take this chance, we might not get another."

A scary thought suddenly occurred to me. "If you were using the Alpha system," I said to Joe, "doesn't that mean they could have tracked you somehow? Maybe picked up your trail?"

Joe smiled. "I wouldn't worry about that. I've got a few tricks up my sleeve."

I shot a questioning look at Sebastian, but he just shrugged. He certainly didn't seem concerned, so I let the issue drop.

He scooped up his coffee and threw back the last sip.

"Well, there's no time like the present." Reaching into his pocket, he removed his phone and tapped the screen several times before lifting it to his ear.

"Hi. My name is Sebastian. Your boss and I have unfinished business. Tell him I will give him a million dollars for five minutes of his time."

* * * * *

Everyone stayed silent on the trip to see Anton. Sebastian's million dollar offer had apparently been enough to buy us entry, but what would happen beyond that was anyone's guess. The closer we drew, the more heavy my stomach felt. I knew I wanted this, to be proactive and take matters into my own hands, but that didn't change the fact that we were driving straight into the lair of a man who, only two days ago, had been trying to kill us. When my brain phrased it like that, it just seemed like a really, really bad idea.

For his part, Sebastian wore a look of grim determination. That comforted me a little. To anyone who was paying attention it said 'fuck with me and you'll regret it,' and I hoped Anton would get the message. I suspected we'd need every little edge we could get.

We were meeting him in the back room of a Kings Cross strip club, which he undoubtedly owned. I'd never really spent much time in the Cross. It's as close to a red light district as Sydney has, and thus the people there are most certainly not my sort of crowd. Between the metric fuckton of makeup that made all the women look like drug addicted clowns and the rather scandalous skin to clothes ratio on display, whenever I visited I wound up feeling trashier just by proximity.

The sight outside the window was no different than I remembered. Even on a weeknight, the main strip was seething with neon light and fake tan. We pulled up outside the club. We'd hired a limo and made a big point of being seen stepping out of it by the two bodybuilders, with sleeve tattoos and steely expressions, who stood guard out front. For appearances, Joe was once again relegated to the role of driver. We had to look calm, in control, and dangerous, rather than desperate and out of options.

"You ready for this?" asked Sebastian.

I took a deep breath. "As ready as I'm going to be."

"Good." He shot me a reassuring smile. "And don't worry, we'll be fine."

I nodded, trying to let some of that confidence seep into my skin.

The men looked us up and down as we approached. They were both as tall as Sebastian, but much wider, which made them incredibly intimidating, by any standards. They looked like someone had taken two plastic bags and crammed them full of walnuts. The larger of them smirked as his eyes rolled over my body, which gave me the sudden urge to go home and take a long shower, but that leer fell away once he turned to Sebastian. My partner was practically radiating danger now, and it was enough to make even these guys pause.

"My name is Sebastian and this is Sophia. We're here to see Anton." His voice betrayed no emotion. 'Just business as usual,' it said.

"Who is Anton?" said giant number one, a look of mock confusion appearing on his face. "I think you must have the wrong place, my friend."

Sebastian didn't even miss a beat. "I don't have time to play games. You know as well as I do that your boss is expecting us."

The man glanced at his partner, who gave a little nod and disappeared upstairs.

The first guy stared daggers at us for several seconds. Apparently he didn't like having his little power trip interrupted.

"I need to search you," he said.

"We're not stupid enough to be carrying here," Sebastian replied.

The guy shrugged. "Then you've got nothing to worry about."

Sebastian waited a few beats then gave a curt nod and stretched his arms out to the sides, gritting his teeth while the guard patted him from head to toe. He wasn't gentle. He almost looked disappointed when he came up empty-handed.

"They'll probably check for these," Sebastian had said to me earlier, nodding towards our guns. "I'd never get one past them, but you just might. Most men struggle to see women as a threat. They never check as carefully."

That had made sense at the time, but as the guard stepped towards me, suddenly the pistol holstered against my inner thigh felt like it weighed a thousand kilogrammes. What would he do if he found it? Laugh and take it away? Or flip out and call his buddies?

He reached out and gave my shoulders and back a cursory check, before moving down my front. He lingered a little below my breasts, the smirk returning to his face, and I had to stop myself from dry retching in his face. I could almost feel the primal frustration simmering below Sebastian's skin, but he restrained himself.

My cheeks started burning as the goon's hands gradually drew closer to the weapon. Despite what Sebastian had said, his search seemed very thorough. He made it as far as the top of my thighs, just inches from the butt of the gun, but as he began to dip between my legs, Sebastian let out a dangerous little growl. "If you want to keep that hand for more than the next three seconds, I suggest you stop there."

The man hesitated, eyes locked with Sebastian. It felt like that night, at my work function, all over again where he'd sent Taylor fleeing with a simple stare. I wasn't sure it was going to work this time — the guard looked like he had something to prove — but after a few moments, he pulled away. I let out a silent sigh of relief. He finished the search in a matter of seconds.

By that point the second thug had reappeared, and he gestured for us to follow him inside. It was early by strip club standards — about six in the evening — so the show hadn't even started yet. The only people in the place were two bartenders milling behind the counter, and a couple of bored looking, scantily clad girls that I brilliantly deduced were strippers. The lack of activity meant that every set of eyes was on us as we crossed the room, which only added to my discomfort.

We were led past another two action movie extras and up a narrow staircase. Unlike the unapologetically tacky stage area, the room we wound up in was fairly inoffensive. It was basically an office, with several chairs, a filing cabinet, and a large desk. The man behind it stood as we entered.

"Welcome," he said. At first glance he didn't appear particularly frightening. He looked to be in his early fifties. Lebanese maybe, or Mediterranean, and with his balding head, slightly retro clothes, and easy smile, he seemed like the kind of guy who'd be found taking his kids to soccer practice on the weekends or playing nine holes with his friends. But the longer I looked, the more I realised how wrong that impression was. It was the eyes, mostly. There was something cold flickering there, something calculating. I got the sense that his friendly appearance was well cultivated, and it could drop away at any moment.

Then, of course, there were the two extra men who had melted across the doorway as we stepped inside. They were doing their best to look bored, but the way they stood, with their jackets casually thrown open to expose their weapons, said that was an illusion too. The message was clear. We weren't leaving unless Anton wanted us to.

"Thank you for seeing us," Sebastian replied.

Anton smiled wider and spread his hands. "When someone makes an offer such as you did, the least a man like me can do is hear him out, wouldn't you agree?"

Sebastian nodded. "I was hoping that would be the case."

"Besides," Anton continued, "it's not often I get a chance to sit down and talk with two people I condemned just days earlier. I had men out there looking for you when you called, you know. And now, here you are. I must admit, I'm curious." The lightness of his tone sent a shiver down my spine. Oh yes, this was a man for whom killing was of no consequence.

But Sebastian appeared unshaken. "Well, like I said, I appreciate it."

"Did you bring what you promised?" Anton asked.

Taking my cue, I lifted the duffel bag I was carrying and dumped it on the table. I'd been quite surprised to find out that a million dollars in cash really did only occupy a few square feet. I thought that was just in the movies.

He didn't even bother to count it. He just unzipped the top and glanced inside. "Wonderful." I figured most people were too afraid to actually try and rip him off.

He gestured for the two of us to sit. "So, what brings you here? I have to say, this is a little unconventional. I'm not conceited enough to say I've never messed up a hit before, but those few lucky souls are usually eager to get as far away from me as possible. You and your lovely lady, on the other hand, have strolled right into my lap."

This was all part of the plan. Intrigue him enough to hear us out, then throw so much money at him that he couldn't resist. I just wished he didn't sound so amused by it all.

"It's simple, really," Sebastian replied. "You have information we want. We're willing to do what's necessary to get it."

Anton laughed. "Nothing is ever that simple in this business. This information, I take it, relates to the people who want you dead?"

Sebastian nodded. "Indeed."

Anton leaned back in his chair and laced his fingers together. "And what's to stop me simply refusing and then having Shawn and Iman here finish the job?" I glanced behind us and saw that the two men now had their hands resting on their pistols. I knew that if Anton gave the order, there would be no hesitation. We'd be dead in seconds. Despite how futile it seemed, I found my hand inching towards the hem of my dress.

"Money, mostly," replied Sebastian.

Anton shrugged. "I already got paid a lot of money to take you out, and that was only half. Now that you have kindly brought yourselves to me, I can get the rest when I report you dead. Not to mention the million you brought along. This has already been an incredibly profitable transaction for me."

"I'm sure we can come up with a sum that will convince you."

The other man studied us for several seconds. "And what about my existing client? I don't know him personally, but I'd hazard a guess that he'll be none too happy with me if I help you. Not to mention the damage he could do to my reputation; client confidentiality and so forth."

Sebastian's gaze turned ice cold. "If you tell us what you

know, I assure you that he won't be around to cause you any problems."

Anton nodded slowly, like he'd just gotten the answer he was expecting. "And what do you think about all this, sweetheart?" he said, turning to me. "You haven't said a word, so far."

That had been part of the plan too. Sebastian was much more familiar with this game than I was, so while I wasn't willing to let him leave me behind, I agreed to let him do all the talking. But I couldn't exactly ignore the question.

"I think it would be in your best interests to take the deal." As soon as the words left my mouth, I realised how they sounded. I hadn't intended to threaten him.

But apparently I wasn't as intimidating as I'd feared, because Anton just burst out laughing. "Is that right? I have to admit, when Leo told me you'd tracked me down, I was a little surprised. That must have taken some serious pull. It makes me wonder." He had that calculating look in his eye again, like he was trying to decide whether we were dangerous or stupid. I realised then that we were dealing with a very smart man. Callous, relentless, but also incredibly shrewd.

Sebastian seemed to recognise an opportunity. "There is more at stake here than you realise, Anton. You don't want to be caught up in the middle of this."

He cocked his head to one side. "Why don't you let me be the judge of that?"

He stared intently at us, weighing our case, our lives reduced to little more than dollar signs on a hypothetical page. Now that we'd played our hand, he knew how much money was really at stake. I assumed he was debating whether to contact his client and start a bidding war. If he knew how powerless we really were, it wouldn't even be a question, but thankfully he was still wary of exactly what we might be capable of.

I did my best to look calm, but my heart was raging like a jackhammer in my chest.

After what felt like a lifetime, he spoke. "Ten million."

"Done," replied Sebastian instantly.

I let out the breath I hadn't even realised I was holding. It was a ludicrous sum — cocktails on a tropical island for all eternity kind of money — but the truth was, we were desperate. We needed him more than he needed us. Besides, I was fairly sure Sebastian could afford it.

Judging by the look in Anton's eye, I think he realised that too. He seemed to be considering if he could get even more.

"I don't have a name for you," he said. "I make it my business to know as little as possible about my clients. It's safer that way, if anyone comes looking." He shot us an ironic grin. "What I do have is the phone number that he originally contacted us on to organise the meet."

Sebastian grimaced. "He won't be using his real phone for this. It's too easily tracked. What about a description? Anything that might help me identify him? I have reason to believe it's someone I'm familiar with."

Anton chuckled softly. "I don't meet them myself. Too risky." He nodded to one of the men in the doorway. "Iman organises the hits."

Sebastian and I both turned to the thug, but he simply shrugged. "He was man. Business man. It was dark, I don't see much." His voice was heavily accented, and it was clear English wasn't his first language. We weren't going to get much out of him.

"Sorry," said Anton.

Sebastian brought his hand up to cover his mouth and

stared into space for several seconds.

"I don't suppose we could just call him? See if you recognise the voice?" I asked.

"Maybe," Sebastian replied. "But then we give away our hand. And he might not answer at all. You said you guys used text messages?"

Anton nodded.

"Then yeah, a call will probably just scare him off."

And then I had an idea. "What does your client know?" I asked Anton. "Did you tell him we got away?"

Anton looked surprised for a moment, but he recovered quickly. "He knows. We had to go in and clean up your mess." He didn't sound even slightly upset about the two men we'd killed. He might as well have been discussing spilt juice. "He was not pleased, although we assured him we were doing everything we could to find you."

"Can you organise another meet?" I continued. "You said he still owes you half on completion of the contract, right? So tell him you've taken us out and you want the rest of your money."

Anton licked his lips. "This is not part of our deal. I would be exposing myself for you."

But Sebastian was nodding now, a hint of a smile on his face. "Fifteen million," he said. "And five more when we have him. Plus you get to keep whatever money he brings."

Anton's eyes widened a fraction. I could practically feel his sense of greed and self-preservation squaring off inside him. He got to his feet, and for one brief terrifying second, I thought he'd changed his mind, but then he extended his hand. "You have a deal."

The tension drained out of Sebastian's face, and he reached up and shook. "I'll have my guy drop the money off." He glanced at the two men behind us. "We'll need to borrow a few of your men."

Anton nodded. "I expected as much. Go with these two. They'll make the necessary arrangements. It's been good doing business with you."

Sebastian stared at him for several seconds, before inclining his head ever so slightly and turning towards the door.

I followed, doing my best not to break into a grin. Somehow, we'd pulled it off. The light at the end of the tunnel had suddenly grown that little bit brighter.

Chapter 13

Sebastian

The meet was set for early evening, in an old warehouse in Macdonaldtown, on the outskirts of Sydney. The location couldn't have been more of a movie stereotype if it tried. Cracked windows, rusted girders, piles of industrial detritus littering the floor. It certainly was empty, though. The roads nearby were completely devoid of people or cars. Movie stereotypes are stereotypes for a reason.

At this point, things were basically out of our hands. Sophia and I sat in the back seat of Anton's car, waiting for the trap to be sprung. Whoever was on the other end of the phone didn't seem to suspect anything. Their text message just sounded relieved. If everything went to plan, in a little while, we'd have our traitor in custody.

I looked over to Sophia, who was staring out the window. She'd handled herself well with Anton. Part of me had wanted to burst out laughing when she'd threatened him, but I'd restrained myself, and somehow we'd bluffed our way through it. We made a good team. She saw the things I missed and she wasn't afraid to speak up when she did.

She glanced up and caught me looking, and a smile lit her face. "Show time, soon." That smile was like a drug to me now. It was my reason to get up each morning. And every time I saw it, I wanted just a little more. When this was all over, I was going to make it my mission to put that smile there as often as possible.

I nodded.

She gazed at me for several seconds, a question poised on her lips. "Do you think this will be the end of it all?" she asked.

I exhaled slowly. I didn't want to dampen the mood of the victory we were about to win here. "I'm honestly not sure," I replied. "Whoever the traitor is, they have a lot of questions to answer. Once we know his motives, and who he's working with, we can plan our next move."

Her shoulders slumped a little, but she tried to remain stoic. "That makes sense."

"Hey," I said, reaching out to brush her cheek with one knuckle. "This is a big step forward. With any luck, they'll crack quickly and tell us everything we need to know. I suspect you'll be back burning the midnight oil at work and getting tanked with Ruth and Lou again in no time."

The smile returned. "I have missed excessive quantities of wine."

"You're allowed to drink more than a glass or two with me, you know."

"And be that embarrassing drunk with the begrudgingly tolerant boyfriend? I don't think so."

"So maybe I'll have more than one or two as well."

She raised an eyebrow. "I didn't realise you did messy drunk."

"I haven't for a few years. But I'm willing to make an exception for you."

She laughed. "That might just be the most romantic offer you've ever made me. It's settled then. When this is all over, we will drink to excess!"

"Deal," I replied.

Another minute passed. "You know, something about this still doesn't sit quite right with me," she said.

"In what way?"

"Well, when you rescued me, you fought your way through a whole house of guards, right?"

I nodded.

"So why did they hire out the killing this time around? Why not use their own people?"

"That's been bothering me too," I replied. "So much of this still makes no sense. Obviously they had their reasons. Maybe we hurt them worse than we thought when we raided that house?"

"Maybe," she replied, although she didn't sound convinced.

"We'll have some answers soon."

"I know," she said.

At that moment, another car appeared at the gate. It was one of the fleet of black Alpha BMWs. I felt something heavy settle in my stomach. Behind those doors was one of my brothers. A man I would have trusted with my life. A man who had betrayed me. I took a deep breath and tried to remain calm.

Through the tinted glass window I watched as the car pulled slowly into the empty lot and stopped about thirty meters away. Iman was standing off to one side, flanked by two of Anton's thugs. He was doing a good job of playing the part. He looked impatient, perhaps even a little bored. Just a guy on another routine pickup.

For a few moments, nothing happened; then the back

door opened and out stepped a man.

Ewan.

Something hot surged in my chest. Until that moment, I think part of me had still refused to accept it. A tiny voice in the back of my head, arguing that there was some other explanation for the way those assassins had surprised us; a hacked security system, or a building flaw we didn't spot. But seeing Ewan there, delivering payment for our deaths, meant that I couldn't lie to myself anymore. The group had been compromised.

It made me feel so damn stupid. I'd always believed the group rhetoric, those wonderful tenants that spoke of using power for the greater good, but now I realised how naive that was. The Alpha Group wasn't some last bastion of nobility. We were as susceptible to greed and self-interest as anyone. I still didn't understand what would possess Ewan to do these things, but I was going to do everything in my power to find out. He would pay for the pain he'd caused.

I looked to Sophia. She had every right to be wearing an 'I told you so' expression, but she seemed to understand the gravity of the situation. Instead, she just shot me a sympathetic smile and reached out to squeeze my knee.

Two Alpha security personnel followed Ewan out of the car, but after a few seconds of hushed conversation, they stayed in place while Ewan began to stride purposefully over the dust towards us. I wondered if the guards had turned on us too, or if they were just doing their job and simply had no idea of the traitorous deal going on right under their noses. I suspected the latter. In our line of work, you naturally see a lot of strange things, and they were taught not to ask questions. Besides, Ewan had kept them purposefully out of earshot. If he had nothing to hide, he'd have brought them in with him. They were probably just here to stop Iman and his men trying anything shady. Only a fool wouldn't tread carefully around Anton Silva.

It felt like it took Ewan forever to cross the empty yard. The animal inside me was raring to simply charge out of the car and let loose with all my rage, until he was just a bloody wreck on the ground, but I knew I needed to hold back. The situation could get messy in a heartbeat, if not handled carefully, and we needed Ewan alive if we wanted any chance of ending this.

When he was a few feet away from Anton's men, he stopped. In his hand he held a plain black briefcase that no doubt contained the rest of Anton's money. "You had me worried," he said. I had the window down ever so slightly, so we could hear everything clearly. "When they escaped the house I thought we'd lost our shot."

Iman smirked. "We find them. Or rather, they find us."

Ewan's eyes narrowed, but before he could react, all three of Anton's men had guns trained on him. The Alpha guys were good. In a split second they were both charging forward and reaching inside their jackets, but they froze as two more thugs emerged from the shadows behind them with weapons raised.

"What is this?" Ewan asked, but there already was a sense of understanding in his voice.

I nodded to Sophia, and we both reached for our door handles. I was expecting fear, but all I saw in his eyes when they fell on us was surprise, followed by resignation. The anger inside me flared. I didn't want him to be okay with what was coming. I wanted him to feel the same terror Sophia had, when he'd taken her from her house. That raw hopelessness of knowing that there was nothing left for him, beyond pain and death.

"This is you, getting what you deserve," I growled, and

before I could stop myself, I clocked him with an enormous uppercut that lifted his body from the ground. I was on top of him, moments later, my fists a blur in front of me, my vision clouded red. There were people yelling behind me, but they were muted and distant. All that mattered was Ewan and the pain I wanted him to feel.

It wasn't until Sophia grabbed my face and yanked my gaze up to hers that the rest of the world came back into focus. "Sebastian, stop! You're killing him!"

I looked down at the crumpled form below me. Ewan's face was a mask of blood and dirt. His hair was matted and his breathing shallow. He wasn't moving.

I closed my eyes and flung myself to my feet. I'd never lost control like that before. It was frightening. And scarier still, it had felt good. I wanted someone to blame for everything that had happened, someone that wasn't myself. And now that someone had finally presented himself, I could finally unleash some of the guilt that was devouring me from the inside. "I'm okay," I said. "I'm okay."

The adrenaline was already fading from my veins. My skin felt hot and my lungs burned. I'd hit him with everything I had.

Sophia leaned down to check Ewan's pulse. "He's alive."

"He's a tough old bastard," I replied.

"We need to get him somewhere soon, though, and check him out. You did quite a number on him."

I nodded. "I'll call in the cavalry."

I walked off towards the corner of the lot, just to put a little distance between Ewan and myself, and pulled out my phone.

"Thomas, I'm going to need a little help here."

* * * * *

"Doctor says he's alright," said Thomas, appearing in the doorway. "You certainly did a number on him."

I grimaced. "That's what Sophia said."

He pulled up a chair and sat down next to me, pouring himself a scotch from the bottle in front of us. It was about two hours since I'd called him, and we were inside a small Alpha complex in the Inner West, which had a couple of rooms fitted to keep prisoners. Holding people wasn't something we did often — we pulled strings, we didn't arrest people — but we liked to be prepared, nonetheless.

He threw back the entire glass in one sip, wincing with the burn, then shook his head. "I never suspected he could do something like this. I mean, he was a bit of an asshole, sometimes, but still. Not this."

"I know," I replied. "Is he talking yet?"

"Not yet. He's awake, but still pretty groggy. It won't be too long, I imagine." Something in the way he was looking at me told me what was coming next. "You could have called, you know. When you disappeared, we all assumed the worst."

I hated that I had to have this conversation, but there was no avoiding it. "I know, but at that point I didn't know who to trust."

A look of hurt crossed his face, and I didn't blame him. He was my friend and he deserved my trust. Then again, I'd thought Ewan deserved it as well. Would I ever be able to fully trust these men again? I wanted to think so, but I suspected there would always be a niggling doubt. I didn't know what to do with that. Maybe I could have lived with it a few years back, but I didn't just have my life to consider anymore. Sophia claimed she was okay with the risks, but that didn't mean I was. I couldn't stand the thought of ever putting her in jeopardy again. She deserved the happiness that came with a normal life, a life of not constantly looking over your shoulder. No matter how hard I tried, I didn't know if I could provide that anymore.

I took the scotch and refilled both our glasses, and we drank in silence for a while. I suspected there would be a lot of this over the coming days. The news of Ewan's betrayal had hit the group hard.

"How's Sophia coping?" Thomas asked eventually.

I felt a ghost of a smile creep onto my face. "She actually seems okay. She's a hell of a lot tougher than she looks."

"I can believe that. Is she still floating around here? I haven't had a chance to talk to her."

"No, I sent her back to the main house with Trey. She wanted to stay, but it was obvious how wiped out she was. Besides, there was no reason for her to be here. At this point, it's just a waiting game." With Ewan in custody, much of the danger had passed, but I wasn't willing to let Sophia go back out into the real world just yet. Now that we knew who the traitor was, she'd be safe in the Alpha house until we could unravel the rest of Ewan's operation. Soon, this whole nightmare would be behind us.

A few minutes later, Marcus walked into the room. "He's awake."

"Does he have anything to say for himself?" I asked.

"Not yet. He wants to speak to you, Sebastian. Said he won't talk to anyone else."

It wasn't a good idea. Despite having had a little time to process his betrayal, I still didn't trust myself to be in the same room as him. Just thinking about it turned my blood to lava. But Ewan was a stubborn son of a bitch. If he wanted me there, he'd hold out until it happened.

"Take me to him," I said with a curt nod.

I followed Marcus into the prison area, and he buzzed me through into Ewan's cell.

He was slouched on the bed in the corner of the room. Thomas and Sophia were right, I really had done a number on him. His face was a mottled collage of purple and yellow. Most of his features were barely recognisable behind the swelling and broken skin. He stared up at me, through his one good eye, still managing to look unafraid.

"So." My voice could have frozen water.

He sighed heavily. "So."

"Let's get this over with. You wanted to see me. Well, here I am."

There was a pause. "I'm sorry, Sebastian."

He couldn't have surprised me any more if he'd tried. My hands clenched tight and I took two big steps towards him until I was close enough to feel his breath on my skin. "Sorry? That's why you brought me in here? To apologise? I don't want your apologies, Ewan! I want answers!" I realised I was shouting, but I didn't care. I needed some outlet for all the anger seething inside me or it was going to come out through my fists again.

He flinched, but his expression remained stoic. "I appreciate that. I'm not going to pretend like that makes it better. All I want is for you to understand; everything I did, I did in the best interests of the group."

"You don't get to decide what's best for the group. That's not your call alone," I spat.

"Maybe not, but I didn't see any other way. She's a liability, Sebastian. And now you are too. The way you reacted when she was taken, well, the council can't afford to have that kind of weakness. Especially not with everything else that's happening. So I did what I thought was necessary."

A trickle of discomfort flowed down my spine. "What do

you mean everything else? You're responsible for everything else."

His eyes widened. "You can't be serious."

"I'm deadly serious. You just admitted to trying to take both of us out, but you expect me to believe you weren't the one who tried to kidnap Sophia?"

He sat up taller, raising his head as close to mine as possible. "I may have been concerned about you for a while, Sebastian, but I didn't do anything about it until that night with Anton's men in the safe house. And as God is my witness, I fucking certainly had nothing to do with Charlie and Simon. They were my friends."

His voice was louder now and full of conviction. It made my head spin.

"So if it wasn't you, who was it?"

"I don't know, but they're still out there."

"You're lying," I said, but I think it was more for my benefit than his. The certainty in his eyes rippled through me.

He studied me. "Maybe I am. Believe what you like, I guess. It makes little difference to me at this point." His eyes narrowed. "But when all of this comes crashing down around you, don't say I didn't warn you."

I stared at him for several seconds, my mind and stomach churning as one. I desperately wanted not to believe him, but what reason did he have to lie? Even if he did convince me, he couldn't think that would earn him clemency. There were no excuses for trying to assassinate a brother. Perhaps he was just messing with me, a last little 'fuck you' for good measure, but if that were the case, he was the best actor in the world. Besides, the sinking feeling in my belly was growing more powerful with every passing second.

The truth was, everything he said made sense. Ewan and I had never seen eye to eye, but his dedication to the group bordered on zealous. Even with what we thought wa[s] right in front of us, I still hadn't really been able to s[ee] doing all of this. Add that to the inconsistencies Soph[i]a had raised earlier in the car, and the doubt only grew.

If he was telling the truth then someone else out there wanted to hurt the group. And that meant we were all still in danger.

Including Sophia.

I was out the door before I knew it, my phone already in my hand. *She's safe. By now she's probably asleep back in the house with armed guards stationed all around her.* But as the phone continued to ring out, a chill rolled through me unlike anything I'd ever felt before.

Ten rings. Twenty.

No answer.

With desperation clutching at my lungs, I hung up and called again. Nothing.

She's not answering because she's passed out. That's all.

I tried Trey's number, but it went straight to voicemail. With my heart beating like a wild drum in my chest, I raced back to find Thomas.

"Who's still at the house?" I asked.

He recoiled as I drew close, like he'd seen something horrifying in my face. "What the hell? What happened?"

"The house," I repeated, barely even hearing his questions. "Who's there?"

He licked his lips. "Jav should still be I think."

I was dialling before he even finished his sentence, and within a few rings, Jav picked up.

"Where's Sophia?"

There was a pause. "Sebastian? What do you mean? She's with you, isn't she?"

I closed my eyes and drew a ragged breath. *This can't be*

happening. "She was coming back to the house with Trey," I said slowly, my voice trembling. "She should have been there an hour ago."

"Trey hasn't been here since he left to meet you."

My hand shot out to clutch the wall as the room spun around me. There could have been other explanations, flat tires and empty phone batteries, but I knew that wasn't the case. I could feel the truth of it right down to my bones. They had her. Again. And it was my fault.

All the signs had been there, and I'd ignored them. And now... oh Christ. I had all the power in the world at my hands, and it wasn't enough. I couldn't even protect the one thing I truly loved.

Trey. He was responsible for this. Whatever destructive plan he had for the group, Sophia was somehow involved. And I'd handed her right to him.

Thomas' expression had slipped even further. "What is it, Sebastian? Is Sophia okay?"

But I couldn't respond. I couldn't even breathe. I felt like I was drowning, like the air around me had suddenly thickened into something my body could no longer process.

Last time I'd had a tail on Sophia from the start. I knew where they'd taken her, and I used that purpose and direction to hone my fear into focus. But this time she could be anywhere. The chance of finding her was next to nothing.

I collapsed against the wall and buried my head in my hands. I realised I was sobbing. I wanted to die. I wanted to curl up into a ball so tightly I just disappeared. My mind was racing, desperately searching for any kind of next move, but it was like trying to catch the wind in my hands. I had no clues. No information. No hope.

And then, my phone vibrated in my hand. The caller ID listed Sophia's number.

Barely breathing, I swiped the screen, and a picture of her flashed before my eyes. She was bound to a slim wooden chair, her mouth gagged, her eyes wide with fear. The caption simply said, "Come alone." It didn't give any directions, but it told me all I needed to know. The room in the background was instantly familiar. It was one of the control rooms in the old Alpha headquarters. The place the two of us had first met.

Trey had Sophia, and he wanted me to come for her.

I felt an icy calm descend over me, a sudden sense of clarity that was almost painfully sharp. Despite how stacked the situation looked, he'd made a mistake by inviting me. I didn't know how yet, but I was going to end this tonight. I'd failed Sophia too many times already.

I wouldn't fail her again.

Chapter 14

Sebastian

There was plenty of muscle waiting for me when I arrived at headquarters; at least ten men wearing suits and impassive expressions. No one commented as I approached, they just stood by with their hands on their holsters as the two closest moved in to search me. The gun strapped under my arm was commandeered without even a frown. I hadn't expected to actually get it past them, but I had to try anyway.

I'd nearly called in the cavalry. Thomas had been flipping out trying to work out what was going on, and it would have been so easy to explain the situation and bring the whole team down here with me. But I took Trey's warning seriously. He wouldn't hesitate to kill her if he got even a sniff of Alpha activity, and I had no idea how far his eyes and ears reached. If he had the right alerts set up, she could be dead before our cars made it a block. I couldn't take that risk.

When the guards were sure I was unarmed, they stepped back and I continued inside. I reached the door that led to Sophia's prison, but I took a moment before opening it to draw a deep breath. I still had no idea how I was going to get us out of this, but I had to remain calm. Blacking out, like I did with Ewan, would get us both killed in a heartbeat. If I wanted Trey and his friends to pay, I had to keep my wits about me. I refused to believe this was the end. After everything Sophia and I had been through, an opportunity would present itself. It had to.

I turned the handle and stepped inside.

Sophia sat towards one side of the room, bound to the chair exactly as she had been in the photo. Her face was puffy and red.

She cried out through her gag when she saw me, a visceral, frightened sound that seemed to echo inside my head. Without even realising what I was doing, I began rushing towards her.

"Uh uh," Trey said, stepping into view and pressing the barrel of his gun right up against her temple. "That's far enough."

Sophia seemed to be trying to tell me something. She'd gone quiet, but her eyes flicked continuously between Trey and the door behind me. I had no idea what it meant. It seemed like all the cards were pretty much on the table at this point.

I turned my gaze to Trey. My anger reared like a rabid dog in my chest, but I kept it leashed. *Focus.*

"You," I said, my voice sharp enough to cut glass.

He blinked a few times, then gave a shaky little bow. "Me."

The room was empty, apart from the three of us. Not that it mattered. He was armed and his goons were just a few steps away.

I studied him for several seconds. He mostly looked like himself. His smile held the same playfulness it always had, but there was something dark seething behind his eyes now too, something off. I had no idea how he'd kept that hidden for so long. "Why?" I asked.

He grinned. "That's the million dollar question, isn't it?"

"Million dollar? So it's money you want?"

"Oh, God no," he replied with a laugh. "Bad choice of phrasing, I guess. No, I may not be worth as much as you, Sebastian, but I'm perfectly comfortable. This is about so much more than that."

The motive behind the attacks had bothered me constantly. I'd never quite been able to make the pieces fit. "You killed Charlie and Aaron."

Trey nodded. "Guilty." He didn't show even the slightest sign of remorse.

"How could you do that? How could you kill your own brothers? We took you in, made you part of the family, and this is how you repay us?"

Trey's expression darkened. "I was never part of the family, Sebastian. I may have the tattoo, but I never had the respect."

I gave a sour laugh. "Respect? Seriously, that's what this is about? Poor little Trey is feeling under-appreciated?"

His jaw tightened. "Even now, you laugh at me." He gave the pistol a little shake. "Not wise to mock a man with a gun."

For a moment, I thought maybe I'd gone too far, but eventually he relaxed.

"You know, my dad used to tell me about you guys, back when I was a kid," he continued. "I know he wasn't supposed to, but he did. He used to tell me the kinds of things you did, the kind of power you had. I used to dream about the day I'd be a part of that. Then you finally invited me to join, and it was the best day of my life. I finally had a chance to prove myself. I spent the next three years busting my ass for the group, but in the end, you know what I had to show for it? The same shitty jobs and cruel jokes as when I started."

"The group is a lifelong commitment, Trey. Things don't happen overnight. You can't just waltz in and expect to be running the show."

"You did. You were, what, twenty seven when they invited you to the council? And dad was just twenty five. Not to mention Marcus. You promote *that guy* over me?" There was something wild in his expression now, something broken. Clearly this wound had been festering for some time. "Dad didn't invite me to the group to be a fucking errand boy. I'm capable of better. I *deserve* better."

"Yeah, well your dad would be turning in his grave if he could see you now." The words left my mouth before I realised I'd said them.

Trey's mouth parted in a snarl and he flung the gun upwards at me, his arm trembling. "You take that back," he hissed. "You take that back! He'd understand. He'd be proud I finally stepped up and did something. He wasn't the sort of man who let other people walk all over him, and neither am I."

"So what is all this then? Revenge? Kill a few group members and make yourself feel better?"

The smile returned to Trey's face, but it was off somehow, crooked, like I was looking at a reflection of it in a splintered mirror. "A little, maybe. But there's more to it than that. That's the problem with the group now. You don't think grand enough. Besides, I'm not the one you should really be talking to about revenge."

I cocked my head. "What's that supposed to mean?"

"Well, as much as I'd love to take all the credit for everything, I have to confess I didn't do it alone. I had a little help from someone who had a slightly more personal stake in all of this." He raised his voice. "You can come in now, babe."

My eyes darted to the door just in time to see a woman step through.

"Hello, Sebastian," she said.

My jaw dropped. It had been years since I'd seen her, but those perfect features and golden locks were unmistakable.

Liv.

For about ten seconds, nobody spoke. She merely smiled, radiating satisfaction while my mouth worked wordlessly. The sight of her made me feel like I was falling, like everything else was zipping past around me. My stomach heaved, my skin prickled, my lungs seemed frozen in my chest. A million thoughts crashed through my head. For a few moments I was actually certain I was dreaming.

"You're alive," I said finally.

Liv let out a little giggle. "As observant as ever, I see." She seemed to have actually dressed up for the occasion. Between the long black gown she wore and the elegant clutch under her arm, she looked like she'd come directly from some kind of fancy charity dinner.

I took a step towards her, my arm twitching forward ever so slightly before I stopped myself. "I saw your body."

"You saw *a* body. Some poor girl they found in an alley in The Cross. OD'd, from memory. A bit of decoration, some creative police reporting, courtesy of Trey, and poof," she made a fist then popped it in front of her, "I was dead."

I felt like my eyes were about to pop out of my head. Turning away, I forced them closed. "Do you know what that did to me?"

Her voice was impossibly cold. "It hurt, I imagine. I hope it did. After the way you left me, you deserved to hurt." She had the same callousness to her demeanour now that Trey did. It changed her. That feminine allure was still there, but it was hardened, tempered by years of bitterness. Two people with huge chips on their shoulders; in a morbid way, they made the perfect couple.

"I left to protect you, Liv." I gestured to the room. "To protect you from all of this."

"I didn't want your protection," she spat. "I wanted you. But apparently that was too much to ask."

I had no idea how I was supposed to be dealing with this. I'd never been so confused in my life.

"So now you're with him?" I asked. "You can't have me, so you take this insecure, traitorous little shit instead?"

Treys snarled and lifted the gun once more, but Liv raised her hand. "Easy, Trey."

She turned back to me. "Yes, I'm with him. After you left, it felt like the world had ended. I gave up my life for you, Sebastian. My dreams. Everything. And then you dropped me without so much as an explanation. When I ran into Trey one day, I was desperately looking for a friend, and at first, that's exactly what it was. But soon enough it turned into something else. He was there for me when no one else was, and so I was there for him too."

She shot Trey a smile, but even that seemed to lack true joy. I wondered how much of their relationship was real and how much was simply fuelled by spite. "Unlike you, he's not afraid to be himself with me. He doesn't treat me like a child who can't handle the truth. He told me who he was, who you were, the way you all treated him, and soon it became clear that our goals overlapped. I realised what we had to do."

I glanced at Sophia, hoping the sight of her would steady me a little. She looked almost as surprised as I felt.

"Well, it looks like you succeeded," I said heavily. "You've got me. Whatever it is you want, Sophia has nothing to do with it. You can let her go now. This is between you two, me, and the group."

Sophia let out a high pitched squeal and shook her head rapidly. I loved that she wasn't willing to leave me behind, but I wasn't going to let her throw her life away for my sake. I'd cost her so much already.

"Well, isn't that touching," Liv replied, her voice dripping with scorn. "Trey told me you two had fallen hard for each other." For the first time, she turned her attention to Sophia. Walking closer, she dipped a hand under her chin, stroking it with one finger. Sophia tried to pull away, but Liv's grip closed around her face, angling her head upwards. Every fibre of my being wanted to stride over there and tear those hands away but, somehow, I restrained myself. We were still poised on a knife's edge. All I could do was watch as Liv appraised Sophia, envy and hatred blazing in her eyes. "To be honest, I'm not sure I see what all the fuss is about."

She turned back to me. "You want us to let her go? Well, that's entirely up to you. Let's see exactly how much you love her." She nodded to Trey.

"It's simple really," he said, gesturing to the Alpha computer terminal at the end of the room. "You log me into the system, we release her."

"I don't understand," I replied. "You want council access to the network?"

He grinned. "Remember what I said about thinking big? No, council access won't be enough I'm afraid. I want the main international database. My employers want access to everything."

"Your employers?"

He spread his hands. "The Syndicate. You don't think we hired all those men ourselves, do you? No, we've had a little support. Once I told them what we could bring to the table, it wasn't difficult to convince them to give me a position in their organisation. A *senior* position."

So The Syndicate *was* involved. I shook my head. The level of betrayal was beyond anything I could have imagined. Trey was quite happy to destroy the entire group, all two thousand years of history, to feed his desperate ego. And Liv, my God. I knew I'd hurt her, but I never dreamed she'd be capable of something like this. Then again, one look at her and it was clear that the woman I'd fallen in love with was nowhere in sight. All that was left was a bitter parody.

I needed to focus. Something he'd said didn't make sense. "Only the current Archon can give you that kind of access. You know that."

He gave a little laugh. "This isn't the time to play games, Sebastian. What do you think we've been doing for the last two years? We've been working out who runs the show. We couldn't see the actual orders of course, but you might be aware that Liv is a little handy with a PC. She actually managed to get a few bits of software piggybacking on your system, while you two were still together, so between that and my basic Alpha access, we've been able to build a pretty accurate picture of the way information in the group flows."

I felt a glimmer of hope, the tiniest hint of light at the end of the tunnel. "And you think it comes from me?"

Trey nodded. "Until a few weeks ago, we had it narrowed down to three. You, Simon, or Charlie. At that point we decided it was more effective to just ask. After giving the others a little more... incentive to tell the truth, they still denied it. Which just leaves you. I have to admit, I was pretty pissed off when you managed to find Sophia the first time. That set us back several weeks. Not to mention Ewan's little stunt." He gestured to the room around us and smiled. "But I guess it all worked out in the end, and that's what counts."

I let my shoulders sag a little, trying to play along. "And

what do you get out of all of this?" I asked Liv.

"Oh, my aspirations aren't nearly as grand," she replied. "Revenge will do me just fine. I'm so glad it turned out to be you. We had our suspicions, even from the start, but we couldn't rely just on those. Now we get to take care of everything all at once. It's so much neater this way."

"And if I refuse?"

"Then we kill both of you, drag you over, and swipe your thumb on the scanner anyway." Her voice was ice cold.

"So why not simply do that to start with?" I asked. "Save yourself all this hassle?"

Liv's expression twisted even further. "I'd rather you were alive to watch it happen."

She'd obviously intended to sound like she was talking about the downfall of Alpha, but the way her eyes narrowed fractionally and darted to Sophia as she spoke said it was more than that. I suspected that the moment I gave them what they wanted, Liv was going to have Trey shoot her in front of me and let me watch her die. My group and my girl in one single move. The ultimate payback for the pain I'd caused her.

Judging by the expression on Sophia's face, she realised the truth as well. Whatever flimsy mask of self-control she'd been maintaining so far had crumpled. She looked absolutely terrified. My mind was madly scrabbling for a way to let her know that we weren't totally out of the game. We were only going to have a tiny window of opportunity and I needed her to be ready, but anything I said would tip our hand. And then it came to me.

"You promise you'll let her go?" I asked.

Liv smirked. "Cross my heart."

My death, on the other hand, was apparently a given, but I'd anticipated that the moment I walked through the door.

I nodded slowly and began moving over to the computer

terminal. Trey followed, gun trained on my chest. "Don't try anything clever. I'm going to bring up the root Alpha portal, and you're going to swipe your thumb for access, then back away. Understand?"

"Yep."

He opened the program. "All yours."

I reached out, and then paused with my thumb over the pad. "You know this is really sweet," I said, gesturing between the two of them. "A real Cinderella story."

A look of confusion crossed both their faces, but I wasn't really paying attention to them. I was staring at Sophia. For a second, she looked perplexed too, but then her eyes lit up as she recognised the safe word she'd picked the first time we were together. Bingo. I tried to draw a line between her and the floor with my eyes, and she gave a tiny nod. It would have to be enough.

"Whatever. Get on with it," Trey said.

I took a deep breath, and pressed down.

And the room was plunged into darkness.

There were two brief cries of surprise, and then the crack of gunfire, but I was already diving to the right. Unfortunately I wasn't fast enough. Heat exploded through my arm and I stifled a scream. It was just a graze along my bicep, but it hurt like hell, and blood was already seeping through the ragged slash in my sleeve. I forced the pain away. I couldn't think about that now. If I went down, so did Sophia, and that was not an option.

A few more bullets slammed into the darkness around me, one passing close enough that I could feel the wind of it on my face. I scuttled along the floor, fumbling blindly for the edge of the desk and pulling myself around it. I hadn't been sure it would work. I'd heard rumours about what happened when someone without authorisation tried to log into the central database, but nobody had ever been stupid enough to try. As I understood it, the whole system, lights, door locks, computers, was now locked down, and an alert had gone out over the network. In a few minutes, Alpha would be showing up here in force. Of course we still had to survive until they arrived.

For a moment I thought that perhaps Sophia hadn't understood my message, but a split second later there was a loud crack, the sound of wood splintering. She'd thrown herself to the ground.

"What the hell, Trey?" It was Liv's voice, and there was a tremble running through it now.

He let out a howl and fired blindly again. "We checked everyone. It had to be you. It had to!" He sounded as though he was talking mostly to himself.

There was a distant commotion outside. No doubt Trey's guards were trying to leap to his defence. But with the system down, all doors into this room had sealed themselves. They weren't getting in any time soon.

Trey had gone quiet now, apparently realising that sound was everything when you were fighting in the dark. Sophia, however, was still audible. Judging by the noise it had made, the chair had broken when she fell, but she still had to extricate herself from the remains. If I didn't distract them, it wouldn't be long before they found her.

It was incredibly disorienting being in pitch darkness. My mind's eye knew roughly where I'd landed, but with no point of reference I felt lost, like I was swimming in a sea of nothingness. I groped behind me where I thought the bookshelf should be, but all I snatched was empty air. I could still hear Sophia struggling to my right somewhere.

"Trey?" said Liv again.

"Quiet," he hissed. His voice had moved now. It was in

the centre of the room. I was running out of time.

Finally, my hands found something solid, the leather spine of a book. I slipped it from the shelf as quietly as I could and then hurled it towards where I'd last heard Trey. I don't know if I struck anyone, but there were two startled screams as the book collided with something, and another bullet zinged into the furniture to my right.

I threw several more, sliding softly along the ground, never staying the same spot. Judging by the yelp of pain, at least one of my projectiles hit its mark, but it wasn't enough. At best I was just delaying them by a few moments. Trey had stopped firing now, knowing the muzzle flash gave him away. I debated simply charging the area where I'd heard him cry out, but I doubted he was staying in one place, either. All that would do is make me an easy target.

I wracked my brain for a way to locate him in the darkness. His mistake had given us a chance, but he still had the advantage. He was armed and I was wounded. Even through the endorphins flooding my brain, my arm was burning like crazy. It wouldn't kill me, but I was already feeling woozy and light-headed. I needed to end this soon.

I fumbled through my pockets looking for anything that might give me an edge. Keys, wallet, phone.

Phone.

And just like that, something clicked into place in my head.

Burying it beneath my jacket, I took a moment to steady my quivering thumb, then I swiped the screen. I had to be quick. I was shielding the light as best I could, but in the pitch darkness it could still give me away. Fortunately, on this unit I only had one number in my favourites list. Sophia's.

I mashed the call button, then locked the screen once more, stuffing it into my pocket to hide the noise. Trey had used her phone to text me just half an hour earlier. I hoped to god he was still carrying it.

After a few agonising seconds, I was rewarded with a chime just a few meters to my left. It was one of those abrasive, pre-programmed ringtones, and it sounded impossibly loud in the blackness. Someone gasped, and I prepared to charge towards the noise, but then another gunshot rang out.

For a moment, I was overcome with confusion. Trey had the only gun, and the shot hadn't come from the same place as the call sound. But then Liv spoke, and I understood.

"What?" Her voice was soft, but full of disbelief, the phone still ringing by her side. There was the sound of something heavy dropping to the floor.

Trey let out a long shriek, and the pain of it was nearly enough to pin me in place. In spite of everything they'd done to us, and the years I'd already thought her dead, I still felt a burst of anguish myself, knowing that she'd been shot. But this was my opportunity, and Sophia's life still hung in the balance. I had to act.

I launched myself into the darkness, hurling my body towards the source of the cry, praying that he was frozen in shock. My shoulder contacted something soft, and there was a grunt, and then we were tumbling to the ground. I wrestled blindly for his arm and two more shots sprayed into the darkness. The sound was loud enough to set my ear ringing. I was bigger than he was, but I was injured, and he was filled with the mad fury of a man with nothing left to lose. My wound was like fire, spreading all across my left side, as I wrestled him for control of the gun. Sophia must have removed her gag. I could hear her calling to me now, desperate and frightened, but I didn't have the oxygen to reply. Every ounce of me was going into this fight.

Somehow, I pulled myself on top of him, wrapping my

hand around his fingers and twisting, sending the gun skidding off into the blackness. He clawed at me with his free arm, snarling wordlessly, but with his body beneath mine, my superior weight came into play, and I managed to keep him at bay. But it wouldn't last. I could feel myself tiring.

With one final surge of energy, I forced my way through his guard, seizing his hair and pulling it up before slamming his head back onto the floor. His body went limp.

And just like that it was over.

As the adrenaline faded, the rest of the world came back into focus. Sophia was still calling for me. "Sebastian? Please, answer me."

"I'm okay," I replied hoarsely. "I'm okay."

She let out a little sob. "I thought he'd shot you. I didn't understand what was going on. Are they...?"

"I don't know." Dragging myself off Trey, I reached out to check his pulse. He was alive. I suspected I'd just knocked him unconscious. I turned towards where I'd heard Liv fall, searching for any sounds of life, but the darkness stayed silent. I couldn't bring myself to try and confirm it. I'd already felt her death once. "I think we're safe," I said.

"What about them?" she asked, and I realised I could still hear the faint rattling of Trey's men trying to break their way inside.

"These doors are deceptively strong. We'll be fine in here until the cavalry arrives."

I searched until I found the gun. It was unlikely Trey or Liv would trouble us again, but I wasn't taking any chances.

By the time I reached her, Sophia had shed the rest of her bonds. She was shivering and, as she burrowed into me, I ran my hand up and down her arm, despite knowing it wasn't the cold that chilled her.

"What happened there?" she asked. "With the lights I

mean? One moment I was sure we were dead, the next you were signalling at me, and then everything just went crazy."

"They had the wrong guy."

"So you're not the leader?"

I shook my head. "Nope."

She actually laughed. It was a tiny sound, but glorious too, and it seemed to release something inside me. "Then who the hell is it? Because I have to say, I was pretty sure it was you, too."

At that moment, there were several gunshots outside. Sophia tensed.

"It's okay. That'll be the good guys."

The door opened, and in stepped Joe, flanked by several guards.

"Well, aren't you two a sight?" he said.

It took her a few moments to understand. "No. Way. *You're* in charge?"

Joe grinned in amusement. "That's perfectly ridiculous, Sophia. After all, I'm just a driver."

But she wasn't having any of it. She turned to me. "Does that make you second in charge?"

"What happened to letting me keep some secrets?" I replied, but I kept my voice light. There was little reason to hide anything at this point.

Soon, the room was swarming with people. Once it had become clear how stacked the odds were, The Syndicate soldiers outside had thrown down their weapons and surrendered. We hadn't lost a single man.

Trey was still out cold, but nonetheless his stretcher was escorted out by an entire team of our best guys. I wasn't sure what exactly would become of him, but I was certain it wouldn't be pleasant. In our laws, the only crime worse than trying to kill a fellow brother is trying to hurt the group itself, and he'd committed both to extreme levels.

Liv, on the other hand, wouldn't have the chance to be punished. Trey's bullet had taken her through the neck, nicking an artery, and she'd bled out, there in the dark. I couldn't even stomach to look at her body. My mind was still reeling from discovering she was alive. Dealing with her death for a second time was the last thing I needed.

At some point, while everything was being dealt with, Sophia slipped away. I found her sitting alone, on a stool, in the crumbling old bar at the front of the complex.

"This is where it all started," she said as I approached. "If I hadn't snuck through the door that night, all of this would have played out differently."

I nodded. I'd never believed much in fate or destiny. The idea of having no control over my life terrifies me to my core. But it was hard not to feel the divine hand of providence in all of this. How else could I have found the soul that so perfectly matched my own? The person that healed the wounds I'd thought were beyond repair?

"Do you regret it?" I asked. "That night?"

One side of her mouth curled up. "Not even for a second."

Part of me thought that made her crazy, but it was exactly what I needed to hear. I pulled up a stool and joined her.

"Is it over then?" she asked.

"I'm almost scared to say yes, but I think, this time, it actually is. We still have a lot of cleaning up to do. I expect once Trey tells us what we need to know, the group will be moving against The Syndicate ASAP. It will be messy, but it needs to be done. With any luck, things will be back to normal in a few weeks."

She nodded, and for about thirty seconds we sat in silence. "I'm sorry about Liv," she said eventually.

I exhaled slowly. "Now *that* was a surprise."

She reached out and took my hand. "Are you okay?"

I didn't answer straight away. After all of the betrayal and deception, and with all of the hurdles still to come, I felt like I mostly definitely should not be okay. But sitting there, with her fingers laced through mine, the worst of our problems finally in the rear view mirror, all I felt was a strange sense of contentment.

"You know, I actually am."

Epilogue

Sophia

The period after it was all over was a bit of a blur. Having learned my lesson, I stayed close to Sebastian for a few days, making sure all the loose ends were tied up.

When we were confident it was well and truly over, Sebastian moved back into his apartment and I went with him. He'd organised a crew to come through and fix the damage to my place, but I wasn't ready to go back there yet. Maybe I never would be. Sleeping alone still held a lot of terrors for me. I doubted I'd fully get over my experiences for some time.

Surprisingly, it was kind of difficult to adjust to a normal life again. After the constant adrenaline, the daily grind felt a little muted, a little dull. I wasn't stupid enough to actually miss all the peril and the betrayal and the men with guns, but there was a certain mystique to having been involved in that clandestine world that, in retrospect, I could almost romanticise.

Despite the fact that we were living together, Sebastian and I didn't get much time alone for the next few weeks. The

Alpha Group was in turmoil over everything that had happened, and there was an awful lot of cleaning up to do. I missed him. After everything we'd been through together, that powerful sense of 'us versus the world', it felt strange to suddenly be apart once more. But I tried to use that time to focus on getting back into my old rhythm. My boss was pleased to have me back, and I assured him that this time it was for good. A few days later, the promotion he'd hinted at officially came through, and I became a senior associate. There was something extra satisfying about the idea of not just being promoted, but stepping into Jennifer's shoes. I had no doubt I'd be up to the task.

I even managed to fit in a little pre-hens night with the girls, which left me with a headache to rival anything Trey had injected me with.

"I knew that skank had to have a secret!" said Ruth, when I filled her in on what had happened with Jennifer.

"Yeah, talk about sleeping your way to the top," agreed Lou.

"The worst part is that it was with Alan," I said, suppressing a shudder. "No promotion under the sun is worth that."

"Well, I'm glad things are back on track," said Lou.

Ruth's smile turned playful. "Speaking of back on track, you hinted on the phone that Sex-On-Legs had a change of heart too."

I grinned at the nickname. "It looks that way."

"Well, that's awesome," she replied. "If any other woman is going to have him, I'm glad it's you."

"You never had him at all!"

Her smile widened and she tapped the side of her head. "Up here I did."

I laughed. "I choose to take that as a compliment."

"And so you should. Just don't go getting any ideas about

diamond rings and screaming toddlers, like this one here," she said, nodding to Lou, "or I may have to disown you both."

"Oh don't be so dramatic," replied Lou. "Once Soph squeezes one or two out and settles down in the burbs, you can come around on Fridays and play charades with us!"

Ruth's face twisted in mock horror.

"I'm not sure there will be much settling in our immediate future," I told them. "After all, I have a partnership ladder to climb."

In truth, I had been feeling a little uncertain about the future, but not for that reason. It was one thing Sebastian and I had yet to talk about. The events of the last few weeks had shown the depth of his feelings for me, and I returned them just as strongly. But now that things were returning to normal, and the adrenaline was fading, the reality of that commitment was sinking in. For better or for worse I'd fallen for a man with some rather unique obligations, and I didn't know exactly what they meant for us. I had no objections about the way our life was now; in fact, it felt a little like I was living in some kind of dream, but was that going to be our life forever? Were the things Ruth joked about permanently out of reach?

All I knew was that I loved him and wanted to be with him, and I figured we'd work it out as we went along.

A week or so later, Sebastian surprised me with another trip to Mi Casa. It was every bit as warm and welcoming as I remembered, with several waiters I only dimly recognised welcoming me like an old friend. The food was incredible again, and since I knew what was coming, I buzzed with anticipation for the entire meal.

As the plates were cleared, and the music started, Sebastian stood and held out his hand. "May I have this dance, my lady?"

This time there was no hesitation. "Certainly, sir," I replied with a giggle.

We danced for what felt like hours, our bodies slowly igniting each other with sensuous rhythm. I half expected him to pull me aside again, to relieve the tension, but much to my disappointment, he restrained himself.

Eventually, he guided me to the edge of the crowd, and then towards the door. I didn't have to ask where we were going.

It was much warmer outside than the last time he'd brought me here, and even up on the headland, utterly exposed to the elements, there was only a soft sea breeze. We settled on the grass, just a few metres from the cliff's edge, and nestled against one another, gazing out over the dark water.

"This really is a spectacular view," I said.

He nodded, but didn't reply, his brow slightly furrowed in contemplation.

"Is everything okay?" I asked.

He blinked several times, then turned to me, his lips curling into a smile. "Everything is perfect." He planted a kiss on the top of my head. "I do want to talk to you about something, though."

"Oh? Let me guess. Thomas has gone rogue and is hunting us even as we speak!"

He laughed. "Not quite." His expression slipped to something that almost looked like nervousness. "I was hoping you'd like to make our living arrangement permanent."

"For real?" We basically were already living together, but nonetheless, the formal acknowledgement was a big step.

"For real," he confirmed. "I love knowing that I've got you to come home to every night. I want to know that I've got that forever."

The word 'forever' sent a warm tingle rolling through my

chest. "You make me sound like a kept women," I replied. "What about the nights where *I* come home to *you*?" I was going for a little sass, but it was somewhat ruined by the sickly sweet smile I couldn't seem to wipe off my face.

He chuckled. "I love those, too."

I made him sweat it for a few seconds, but the truth was he'd had me from the moment he opened his mouth. Hell, he'd had me almost from the moment we met. There was no want left in our relationship now, only need. I needed him like I needed air, and I couldn't imagine going home to a house without him either.

"Of course I'll move in with you."

He let out a long breath and his face lit up like a Christmas tree. "That's what I wanted to hear."

"Although I have to say, Ruth's probably going to have an aneurysm. I'm the last domino standing, and I have no doubt she'll see this as a sign that the end is nigh."

"The end?"

"You know, marriage, kids, impractically fluffy pets. To Ruth that stuff is the end."

He laughed. "I see."

"No pressure from me — these hips won't be passing any little bundles of terror for at least a few more years — but if you plan any more big changes, give me a little notice so I can ease her into the transition, okay?"

His expression lost a little of its amusement. "Well actually, there is one other thing I wanted to mention."

"Oh?" I said cautiously.

There was a long pause. "I quit."

Something shifted in my stomach. "Quit? What do you mean quit? I thought that wasn't allowed."

"Well, maybe that's not quite the right word. Rather, I asked Joe to fire me."

"He can do that?"

Sebastian shrugged. "He's in charge. He can pretty much do what he wants. Call it a perk of knowing the boss."

"And he was okay with it?"

Sebastian gave a surprised little smile. "Yeah. He actually seemed happy to do it."

I shook my head slowly, trying to come to grips with what he was saying. I couldn't deny that the idea of having Sebastian all to myself filled me with joy, but I didn't want that at the expense of his happiness. "Wow. I appreciate the gesture, Sebastian, but are you sure? I mean, we're doing okay now, aren't we? Things don't need to change."

"I'm not worried about the ninety nine percent of the time things are going fine," he said. "I'm worried about the one percent that they're not." There was pain on his face now. "Everything that happened recently has made me realise a few things. I'm not sure I'll ever trust the group like I used to. Those men are my friends, and they'll remain that way, but they also swim in dangerous waters. You know that as well as anyone." He took one of my hands in his and raised it to his mouth, brushing soft kisses across each knuckle. "Maybe nothing like that will ever happen again. But I'm not willing to risk it. I'm not willing to risk you."

The look on his face, the fierceness, the fire, the love, it rippled through me. But still, this felt like too much. "I don't know, Sebastian. I mean, this is who you are, this is what you do. It may not make for an ideal relationship, but we can make it work. I never expected you to give up your life for me."

"This isn't me giving up my life, Sophia," he said. "This is me beginning it."

I could only shake my head and grin like an idiot as my heart melted into a puddle in my chest. "Well, how can a girl argue with that?"

He pulled me in for a kiss and, for a while, I lost myself in his lips. There was a strange sensation blossoming in my chest, one that took some time for me to recognise. Hope.

He was right.

Everything was perfect.

Thanks!

Thank you so much for reading. I hope you enjoyed the story. Writing this series has been an amazing journey, and I have each and every one of you to thank.

When I was writing the series, I was considering a couple of options for the epilogue. Basically, I saw Sophia and Sebastian's HEA going one of two ways when the dust had settled. One of them was a lot of fun, but I ended up deciding that they just wouldn't make that decision after everything that happened. So in the final version of the story, I went with the more believable (and sweeter) option.

But since the other option was fun to consider, I decided to release it for people on my mailing list as an exclusive little bonus. It doesn't in any way impact the real end. It's just a deleted scene that I thought some people might enjoy. If you want to see how Sophia and Sebastian's lives could have been, all you have to do is sign up to my newsletter (just go to my website, http://mayacross.com, and click 'newsletter'). Once you've put in your email address, it will send you a confirmation link. Click that and you'll receive an email with a link to the bonus scene. If you're already on my mailing list, the link was included in the mailout I sent when Unlocked launched, so look back through your inbox. It would have arrived around the 18th of August.

I'll be releasing several bonus scenes exclusively to my email list over the coming months (I really want to write the Mi Casa dance scene from Sebastian's POV), and I am also planning to start a monthly gift voucher giveaway for my mailing list fans, so there's lots of reasons to stay in touch! I promise not to share your email with anyone else, and I won't clutter your inbox (I'll only be mailing when there's something important like a book launch or sale).

Also just a friendly reminder that if you did like the story, the best way you can show thanks and help me keep producing more work is to leave a review on the site you bought from. You don't have to compile an epic three page analysis; even just a single line and a star rating helps. Anything that lets other people know you enjoyed it. It's a little thing, but it makes a big difference to writers like me.

Thanks again!

About the Author

Maya Cross is a writer who enjoys making people blush. Growing up with a mother who worked in a book store, she read a lot from a very young age, and soon enough picked up a pen of her own. She's tried her hands at a whole variety of genres including horror, science fiction, and fantasy, but funnily enough, it was the sexy stuff that stuck. She has now started this pen name as an outlet for her spicier thoughts (they were starting to overflow). She likes her heroes strong but mysterious, her encounters sizzling, and her characters true to life.

She believes in writing familiar narratives told with a twist, so most of her stories will feel comfortable, but hopefully a little unique. Whatever genre she's writing, finding a fascinating concept is the first and most important step.

The Alpha Group is her first attempt at erotic romance.

When she's not writing, she's playing tennis, trawling her home town of Sydney for new inspiration, and drinking too much coffee.

Website: http://www.mayacross.com
Facebook: http://facebook.com/mayacrossbooks
Twitter: https://twitter.com/Maya_cross

Made in the USA
Lexington, KY
19 August 2014